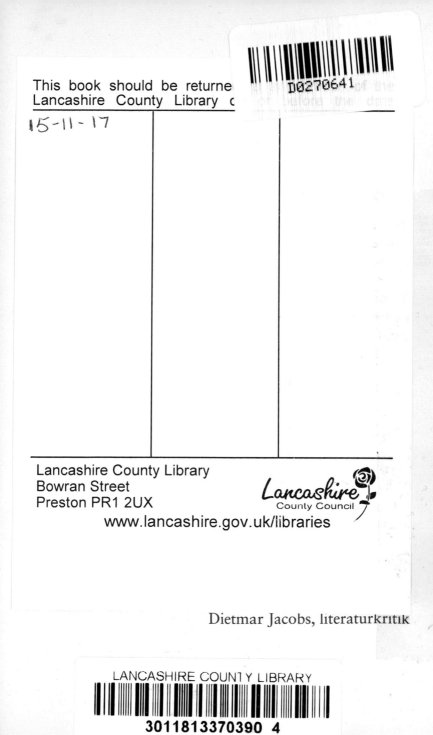

Dietmar Jacobs, literaturkritik

'Smyth is a febrile and original talent!'

The Times

'An absolutely dreadful book in the best sense of the word.'

TW, *Kaliber38–Leichenberg*

'Smyth is shiveringly superb!'

Image Magazine

'The main topic of this book, even before its crime element, is the appalling circumstances under which orphans in Irish children's homes suffered. The Catholic Church had sinned against these young boys and girls so abominably that the Irish Prime Minister even apologised for the collective failure of society in 1999.'

Hans Jörg Wangner, *SZ*

'Smyth has written a short, fast-moving story that I'm sure will haunt me for a long time. Smyth can really write. He says a lot with no wasted words. Adrian McKinty has some rough stories to tell and he does it well but BLOOD FOR BLOOD is even stronger stuff. This is a book to be read and thought about. I recommend it to anyone who likes a good mystery with characters like no other in any mystery I've yet to read.'

Crime Always Pays

BLOOD FOR BLOOD

BLOOD FOR BLOOD

J.M. SMYTH

BLACK & WHITE PUBLISHING

First published 2016
by Black & White Publishing Ltd
29 Ocean Drive, Edinburgh EH6 6JL

1 3 5 7 9 10 8 6 4 2   16 17 18 19

ISBN: 978 1 78530 046 2

This novel is a work of fiction. The names, characters and incidents
portrayed in it are of the author's imagination. Any resemblance to
actual persons, living or dead, or events is entirely coincidental.

A CIP catalogue record for this book is available from the British
Library.

An Everest of love for my darling wife Phyll, my soulmate since we were sixteen. To know you're always with me is all I'll ever need.

And for my mum, Lily, and my granny, Maisie, the two greatest and most supportive influences in my life. If your examples were followed there wouldn't be an unloved or neglected child on the planet.

AUTHOR'S NOTE

The Catholic Church ran Irish orphanages for most of the twentieth century. In the 1990s they were exposed as the 'gulags' of Ireland. Justice was removed and there was nowhere to go for it. Some survivors meted out their own. The Irish prime minister made a statement in May 1999: 'On behalf of the state and of all citizens of the state, the government wishes to make a sincere apology to victims of childhood abuse for our collective failure to intervene, to detect their pain, to come to their rescue.'

RED DOCK

Wanna be a millionaire? Then don't work for a living. Fifty years of that crack and before you know it some joker's digging a hole and lowering you into it. 'Oh, he was such a nice man. He'll be sorely missed.' A load of bollocks. Take my advice: he who works last lasts longer.

'Aye, well, it's all right for you,' I hear you say. 'But how do we make a million?' Fair question. You could try kidnapping, but I wouldn't advise it. I've never seen one yet that hadn't got something wrong with it. Grabbing the victim's easy enough; collecting your wages is the hard part. Either the victim calls attention to himself by being unreasonable and trying to escape or there's a lot of extra coming and going where you're hiding the bastard, and the next thing you know the TV's running it and some nosy neighbour's saying to herself, 'Here, hang on a minute,' lifting the phone and it's, 'Fuck me, the cops are surrounding the place.'

Nah, the only way to kidnap somebody is to get rid

of them as soon as you grab them. No nosy neighbours, no hideout, no coming and going, nothing to worry about. These days it pays to be streamlined.

So I told Charlie Swags that as soon as the baby was snatched, it was to be taken out of the city. (The last thing you want is some squealy kid knocking about the place.)

Then I sent its mother a note; the usual stuff – NO COPS, BRING CASH (in this case a hundred grand) – and the following morning gave her a call. She had to be sitting with her hand on the phone if the speed of her was anything to go by.

Here she was: 'Yes? Yes? Hello? Hello?'

She must've thought I was deaf. I could just imagine the lads there with her whispering, 'For fuck's sake, missus, will you give us a chance to get the trace going?'

'Mrs Winters?'

'Yes, this is Mrs Winters.'

'You want your baby back, you bring the money to Kilreed today at two o'clock. Wait in the phone box outside the post office. And come alone.'

It's hard to tell from a few words, but I got the distinct impression she was suffering with her nerves. Maybe she wasn't sleeping well.

Of course you're saying to yourself by now: how's he gonna collect the money if he's no baby to hand over? Simple: only kidnap when you want to drive the victim's loved ones round the twist. As a diversionary tactic – never for money.

2

Not that she had any. Not on her husband's wages. She was probably driving him nuts with the 'I want my baby' routine. Y'know what women are like. He was probably wishing they were like tape recorders and came with a pause button.

She wasn't a bad-looking woman though: late twenties, popcorn hairstyle. Brave pair of tits on her too – I've seen smaller arses. Not that I fancied her. In women, I wear a size ten; she had to be a fourteen at least. My only interest in her was that her husband had got in Charlie Swags's way, and I needed him to get in somebody else's.

So at two that afternoon I was in the attic office of a hotel, binoculars in hand, looking down at Mary Winters as she went into the phone box in the village of Kilreed to take my call. She was looking very red around the eyes – probably something to do with the wallpaper paste Swags's men had squirted into them when she'd stepped out of the lift of an underground car park and had junior snatched out of its carrycot. They'd mixed citric acid with the paste, by the way. They tell me Optrex is good for getting rid of it, but you need gallons of the stuff. A hospital's better.

'Turn left at the corner,' I told her, 'then left again at a sign that says "Whites". Follow the lane till you come to a farmhouse.'

I watched her arrive. Whites' farmhouse was less than half a mile from where I was. She'd be bugged of course, and the law wouldn't be far away, waiting to pounce when I handed over the baby. That's how they'd be seeing it. They have training for this sort of carry-on, so they can get their man.

She got out of her car, y'know, looking around the farmyard to see what the story was – no doubt expecting me to pop out from behind the barn or whatever – and heard what I wanted her to hear – the sound of her baby roaring and crying in the farmhouse, then the phone ringing just inside the open front door. I was giving her another little call to see how she was getting on.

'Put down the attaché case and go up and get your child,' I told her.

After that I couldn't tell you what happened exactly. I couldn't see inside. But I'd say she went on in through the hall and looked up and saw an infant in a body harness dangling from the hatch into the attic, where I'd left it.

She was very controlled, to be fair to her. No 'Oh my God's, or 'Look at my poor baby' crap. All I heard coming down the phone was a distracted wail of relief, then the sound of the case hitting the ground and her running up the stairs, the stepladder creaking as she climbed up to save her baby, only to find a doll dressed in the clothes it was last seen wearing, and her going into hysterics – which was nothing to the screams that came out of her when she climbed up into the attic and saw a recorder playing the tape I'd made of her baby crying and realised that she was going home alone – aaagghh! – and wailing, 'Where's my baby? Where's my baby? Where's my bay … be …' and breaking down in tears.

Whether or not the case contained the cash, I couldn't

say. The law had no doubt come up with it for the occasion. They have contingency funds, y'know, for unforeseen eventualities.

Anyway, I heard the clatter of her flying back downstairs to the phone, then coming at me again with her 'Where's my baby, where's my baby? Please tell me where my baby is' routine.

'You were told not to involve the cops.'

'But my husband's a Guard. How could I not tell him?'

He was a detective sergeant. Chilly Winters. One of the Garda Síochána's finest. Trained to notice if *his* kid'd been kidnapped. He could notice whatever he liked as long as it wasn't me.

'I can't show my face with him in on it.'

'What was I supposed to do? She's his daughter. What was I supposed to do-oo?'

'Find some way to keep him out of it.'

'How could I? Tell me. Plea-ease. I'll do anything you say.'

'I'll have a think and get back to you. I can't say fairer than that. Bye now.'

'No, wait. Tell me where my baby is. Please tell me where my baby is. Please. Please ...'

A monk's fancy woman could have been breastfeeding it for all I knew.

Oh, I meant to say, as far as their investigation was concerned, the Gardai would carry out their inquiries, you know the way they do – locate my vantage point as the only place the farmhouse could be seen from

5

across the village rooftops by tracing the phone I was using, which had only one set of prints on it, belonging to a man called Ken Varden, who was connected to the hotel. That way they'd go after him instead of me. He had a beef against Chilly Winters and vice versa. Winters had reason to suspect him for this. Everything would fall into place. Except Ken Varden. He'd already fallen into another place.

And Mary Winters is still waiting for me to get back to her.

So forget kidnapping. There's plenty of other ways to make money. If you're prepared to do what I do: make your experiences work for you.

As far as Mary Winters' daughter was concerned, well, no point in wasting a perfectly good baby.

And I had a personal use for it. One that had nothing to do with Charlie Swags or anybody else. The real reason I had taken it.

Yeah, well, that's the way it goes.

I went to see my brother Conor about it.

Conor was doing all right for himself – owned a thatched cottage at the gate to a long drive that led up to where he was having a big house built, horses and cattle in the fields, new motor at the door. Gorgeous.

He was lunging a horse when I arrived. So I just leaned against the fence and enjoyed the feel of the place. I love watching horses. Maybe I'd have taken them up too if things had started off differently. I think it's in the blood, y'know. Still, what with the old leg fucked, not much I could do about it now. If you saw me getting on a horse you'd think I'd been thrown by one. Odd how two guys from identical backgrounds can end up so far apart though. That's what an accident of birth does for you, I suppose.

Some horseman, my brother. In different circumstances I'd probably even be proud of him. Ah well, back to why I'd come.

He unclipped the bay, slipped off its bridle and let it run loose.

'Nice horse,' I said.

'Not bad.'

'Red Dock's the name.'

'Conor Donavan. What can I do for you?'

'I'm looking for a friend of mine – a girl I knew in London – by the name of Anne Donavan. The priest in the village said I'd find her here.' It was bullshit. He couldn't know her. She was a figment of my imagination. And I hadn't seen a priest in years. Religion never added up for me.

The only Anne Donavan Conor knew was his daughter. She was the main reason I'd come. I wanted to get something straight in my mind about her. 'She's never been in London,' he told me. 'She's below in the cottage, if you want to have a word with her, but she'll tell you the same – she's the only one by that name round here.'

Helpful sort of a brother. Strange standing talking to him without him knowing who I was.

Anne didn't know me either when I put the same bullshit to her. I was three feet away from her but I could've been the Man in the Iron Mask for all she knew. And yet I was her uncle. Funny how people's perception of each other based on the information they hold rules out what would otherwise form instant recognition of a fellow family member. That old saying 'He comes from a close family' applies only if they know who you are.

'Everything is relative,' a guy once said to me. I didn't know what the fuck he was talking about. I was only ten. 'Except for you,' he said. 'You're not relative. Not even to your relatives. No one gives two fucks about you, and I can do with you whatever I like.'

That's me – not relative. What I do doesn't count. Who gives a fuck?

'Sorry I can't help you,' Anne said.

She was helping me just by standing there with no wedding ring on her finger and being old enough to have a baby (seventeen, I'd say – three years younger than me). I'd need someone to say he'd delivered it of course. I had it in mind to make Anne the mother of Mary Winters' baby. Well, every child needs a mother. Call it the sentimentalist in me. Like everything else, it's all a question of getting the paperwork right.

'I wonder if it's worth trying the local doctor,' I bullshitted on. 'He might know the Anne Donavan I'm looking for.'

I knew there wasn't another one. But I double-check every detail.

She didn't look as if he'd hold out much hope. Tight-knit farming communities, where everybody knows everybody else, y'see. She gave me directions to the guy who'd delivered me – Doctor Skeffington.

'He's the only doctor round here,' she said. 'He sits from four till six.'

'Thanks.'

I didn't go in to see him – the medical query I had in mind was best handled outside of normal visiting hours.

So I watched until he came out of his surgery and drove away in a Ford Cortina. New one, by the look of it. He was being called out. To a farm, as it happened, along a country lane wide enough for only one vehicle. Nice and quiet.

I reversed my car into the lane and sat trying to pick a few winners for the next day's meeting until I saw his headlights coming back on and his car pulling out of the farmyard. Then it was just a case of opening the bonnet and waiting till he pulled up behind me. Considerate sort: he switched off his main beam so it wouldn't blind me, got out and came round to where I was leaning over the engine looking browned off. Tall, skinny guy he was in a tweed suit, with a white moustache and hardly any hair.

'Sorry about this,' I said. 'Just conked out.' A new Merc, it was. 'You'd think they'd be more reliable. Can't depend on anything these days.'

'Sure now, these things happen,' he said. 'And usually on a night like this.' He buttoned up his car coat.

Seemed pleasant enough. I always liked that about country people. They're so easy-going. Break down in the city and the cunts are ready to beat you out of the road.

'You're not going back towards the village?' I asked him.

'I am.'

'Any chance of a lift?'

'Jump in.'

'Great. I better not leave her blocking the road.'

He gave me a shove. Didn't take much. I'd chosen the brow of a hill, to save our backs, y'know. Just a matter of freewheeling her down onto the main road and in tight to the hedge then getting into his passenger seat.

'Now,' I said and came out with some tripe, letting on to thank him.

'Ah, not at all,' he said and set off, both hands on the wheel, eyes front. Careful driver. You'd have thought he was taking his driving test.

'You're a doctor, I see.' His bag was at my feet.

'I am.'

'Busy?'

'Sure now. January. You know yourself.'

I did indeed. I'd only just got over a sore throat. Had to take antibiotics. 'You know,' I said, diving straight into why I'd swung the lift, 'something's always interested me, and maybe you can help me out.'

'What's that?'

'Well, a mate of mine's wife had a baby born in the house and when he went in for its birth certificate, they just handed it over. No proof required. I mean how did they know he was telling the truth? He didn't have the baby with him.'

'When a baby is born at home, the attending doctor or midwife rings the maternity ward dealing with that area – St Martin's in Dublin, in the case of Clonkeelin – and the birth goes on the register. The registrar's office only has to ring the maternity ward in question to confirm before issuing the certificate.'

'In that case, you wouldn't do me another favour?'

'What's that?'

'Ring St Martin's and tell them you've just delivered a baby.'

'Eh? What baby?'

'A girl.'

'What girl?'

I think taking a revolver out of my inside pocket gave him a hint. It affected his driving anyway. One look at it and he nearly ran into a hedge. 'Watch the road now,' I said. 'We don't want to be calling any doctors.'

He was a steady old boy, all the same, and soon got a hold of himself. Didn't look like he was shitting himself or anything. Just like I had his undivided attention. Interesting how people's faces react to this type of carry-on. Some the blood drains out of. Though it doesn't always take a gun to make that happen – footsteps approaching the dormitory after lights out used to have the same effect; you get to know the sound of certain footsteps – while others' ability to make spit runs out on them. The doc was fast becoming the latter. From then on he sounded like he could murder a drink.

Still, as long as it didn't affect his voice too much. It was his voice I wanted. More than likely St Martin's would recognise it. Of course I could always ring them myself, saying I was Doctor Skeffington, and report a birth, but what if I hit on a nurse who knew him? She'd know right away I wasn't him. Whereas if he rang, it would all seem authentic.

'Look,' he said, 'I don't know what all this is about, but—'

'No buts, Doc. Just pull in at that phone box.' (I'd clocked it on the drive out, for the return trip.) 'All you have to worry about is making the call the way you always make it. Then you can go home.' I find it best not to give people too much information when their lives are under threat. That way they can tell themselves that everything will be OK if they simply do what they're told. It's bullshit of course, but that's self-preservation for you.

He hit the brakes.

'In you go,' I said and went in behind him. 'Tell them Anne Donavan's just had a baby.'

'*Anne Donavan?* But Anne's not even pregnant.'

What the fuck did that have to do with anything? Some people, I dunno, you have to tell them a dozen times. 'Make the call, Doc, and stop fucking about. I haven't got all night. C'mon, move. And don't forget to tell them her address.'

He did what he was told, fumbling with the dial and pressing the 'A' button a couple of times when the hospital answered. 'Hello, this is Doctor Skeffington …

I've just delivered a baby to Anne Donavan, Clonkeelin …' All that crack.

'A girl,' I whispered.

'A girl,' he told whoever was on the other end. 'A baby girl.'

I'd decided to call the girl Frances incidentally. Frances Anne Donavan. I like the name Frances. The 'Anne' part was for the kid to latch on to as a sign when she grew up. Her birth had now been registered by Anne Donavan's own doctor.

'OK,' I said, 'back in the car.'

'Can't I go now?'

'You don't expect me to limp home, do you?' What kind of doctor was he? It must've been the guts of ten miles back to Dublin. Not that I was going there right away. Besides dealing with him, I couldn't leave my Merc lying around for Winters to find and think: fuck me, that's Red Dock's car. Wonder what it means. You know what cops are like, always wondering what stuff means.

I jumped in the back and told him where to go. Then came a spot of reminiscing. 'You don't remember me, do you?'

'No. No, I don't.'

I'd put on a bit of weight since our last meeting. 'You made a similar phone call the night I was born.' No gun needed that night.

'The night *you* were born?'

'You delivered me. My mother was Teresa Donavan. She had twins.'

I don't think he was much into reminiscing. He was more concerned about his future. But it was coming back to him. Not his future – it was taking its last trip. The memory. Not a pleasant one, if the gob on him was anything to go by.

'Which one of us was born first?' I asked. The lady in question having since departed with the info, he was probably the only one left who knew.

'Ah …'

'Sean or me?'

'Ah …'

'Quit with the "ah"s, Doc. You're not checking my tonsils. Which of us was born first? Sean or me?'

'Ah …' Shit. He hadn't given it much thought of late. 'In the name of God, why are you asking me this?' was the sort of crap he was expecting me to put up with.

'Answer me.'

'But I don't know.'

'Was Sean first or was I? I'm Robert, by the way, in case you don't recognise me. Nice to see you again after all these years. Which of us was born first? It's a simple question. Me and Sean used to lay bets on it. He used to bet me he was. I used to bet him I was. Typical kids' stuff. So who was born first – me or Sean?'

'I don't know, as God is my judge. It was too long ago.'

'Think, man, think. How many sets of twins did you deliver then never lay eyes on again, for fuck's sake?'

It was no good. He was straining for an answer but couldn't latch on to one. By this stage, if he had, it would only have been his way of attempting to appease me. Therefore I wouldn't have believed him. That's the trouble with this lark – nobody bothers to remember fuck all about you. Fuck it. I'll give you the benefit of the doubt, Sean. You were born first.

'Why did she give us up? And don't give me any doctor–patient confidentiality crap.'

'But you don't understand. I was standing in for my predecessor. He was off sick. I was only here for a few months. I loved it here. When he retired five years ago I bought his practice. I had always practised in Dublin. I wanted to end my working days in the countryside. I ... I ...'

Fuck it – this wasn't working out at all. Nobody lies with a gun in their neck. I'd felt sure he could help me. I didn't ask him who my father was. He wouldn't have known that either. If he had, he'd have known why we'd been given into care. 'Care.' There's a word if I ever heard one. I looked it up in a dictionary once. It had a lot of definitions – but not the one that applied to me and Sean.

'Take the next left.' It had a long stretch of narrow road that rounded a sharp corner. 'And hurry up, for fuck's sake. Hit the throttle.' I doubt he'd ever hit it as hard.

I couldn't leave him to talk.

I slammed his head down onto the wheel hard enough to knock him out, then dived down behind both seats a split second before the car smashed into the high wall bordering the field that formed the corner. It hit it a fair old whack too. Hard enough to make the back end leave the ground. If I'd been in the front, I'd've wrecked my hair smashing through the windscreen. What was left of his was already wrecked. I was all right though, no damage done. Just a pain in my side. That's what I get for not wearing a seat belt.

I got out and opened the bonnet.

The trouble with this method is that sometimes the 'whack' fucks the bonnet catch and it won't open. Makes it hard to pour petrol over the engine. Half a Lucozade bottle's usually enough. You have to be quick though. No need to strike a match – the heat of the engine sets it alight then it's drop the bonnet and get the fuck away from it as fast as you can.

The only thing I didn't like about this was that the law'd find out he was a careful driver and wonder if foul play had been involved. On the plus side, this was the country, and sheep are forever darting in front of cars. Maybe he got caught out swerving to avoid one. The bump on his head would be consistent with hitting the wheel on impact, leaving him unconscious to be barbecued. And although cars rarely burst into flames on impact, the fuel pipe would be destroyed and forensic wouldn't be able to tell conclusively what had happened.

Which left the little matter of my prints. They were all over the inside of the car. It goes without saying that they'd end up as charred as the good doctor. That's what he gets for giving people lifts. I waited for a few minutes to make sure he didn't come round. Even if he had, he wouldn't have survived long enough to get out anyway. I'd nearly wound down the back-door window before the impact to let the air in on it. Air would've got the flames going faster, but the law might've wondered why it had been left open on a winter's night. Had he been carrying a passenger? Who? It doesn't do to give the bastards too much to think about. Besides, you're only talking about getting it going faster by a matter of seconds.

Leaving the windows closed of course meant that the heat from the flames made pressure build up inside, and the only way it could escape was by blowing the windows out. I legged it way before that happened, empty Lucozade bottle in hand. Can't leave evidence like that lying about. I have to take my time when it comes to legging it. That's why I always have to be choosy when it comes to the likes of this. I can't do anything if it involves lifting. I heard the glass blowing out though. Not much of a bang. More of a boomph. I doubt the doc'd heard it or gave a fuck. He was approaching the rare stage. Another ten minutes and he'd be well done.

The following morning I went straight to the Registrar of Births, Marriages and Deaths in Dublin and applied for a birth certificate for Frances Anne Donavan and gave them the mother's details. They phoned the maternity ward, did their confirming and issued the cert. Anne Donavan now had a baby called Frances she didn't know about.

Didn't matter: she wasn't gonna bring it up. It had

gone from being a Winters to being a Donavan, and now it was in for another name change. I'd already taken it to experts in that department.

The day the kid was snatched by two of Charlie Swags's finest, I was waiting in the lower ground floor of the same car park. They bunged it into the back seat and I drove straight to the west of Ireland to an orphanage in Connemara. It cried for most of the 200 miles. I got some of it on tape for Whites' farmhouse attic. Mustn't forget the special effects. It was only when I arrived at the orphanage that I noticed what was making it howl. Some of the paste that had been squirted into Mary Winters' eyes had gone into its left eye, and had left it red raw.

I put a note in its shawl saying 'I'm sorry. I'm so sorry. Please take care of my baby. They won't let me keep her.' The nuns would believe it was illegitimate, and the note would indicate the mother couldn't raise it by herself because of the shame it would bring on her family.

Thanks to all that stigma stuff they'd attached to illegitimacy, dumping unwanted kids was easy. I couldn't have done it without them.

And the reason I'd chosen this particular orphanage: I didn't want the kid found. It was in Connemara and Connemara was a generation behind Dublin. In some instances, ten of a family eking out a living on a few acres, living in a cottage with a tin roof and mud floor, no electricity or running water – let alone a TV to see the news – was not common, but not unheard of either. And Irish was spoken as much if not more than English. Dublin news wasn't exactly widespread in that part of the country. A too-easy view to take, I know. Connemara was hardly the Amazon jungle. People there would hear of it. I mean we're talking about a cop's kid being kidnapped. Then again, on the face of it, it was just another little baby girl born into a world where she wasn't welcome, dumped on the steps of a home in the middle of the night with no birth cert. And I knew that the Church had made a career of keeping babies. I knew the system – that keeping her gelled with what I knew about them.

I forgot about the kid for a while after that. Then I took to renting a cottage in the village she was near for the occasional week over the next few years and got on nodding terms with a couple of the nuns. In the summer months the kids worked the land they had there, growing vegetables and stuff. They used to sell them to the public, and I was a customer. Gradually I got to know some of the kids by sight. One in particular stood out. At my reckoning she was just coming on six years of age, and she had a birthmark just above her elbow, which I had searched for the night I'd brought her there, to identify her to me later on. But that wasn't what made her stand out. She had what had turned out to look like a second birthmark – a blotch in the corner of her eye. The wallpaper paste had scarred her. A very minor mark, not unattractive, strangely enough, but it looked permanent. The nuns hadn't treated it, and it had burned her.

So I'm standing there in my walking gear, as if I'd holidayed in the area for that purpose, complimenting this nun on their set-up, and admiring the rows of meticulously weeded vegetables, when the girl came over with a basket of carrots she'd dug up. She emptied it onto a cart then turned to the nun.

'Can I give Jack one, Sister?' she asked.

Sister smiled like the Virgin Mary at her and the girl gave the donkey the carrot, patting him and all that, saying, 'There's a good boy, Jack.'

Not to be too obvious about singling her out, I asked a couple of other kids their names. 'Gemma Small' and 'Rebecca Donagher' they said.

'And what's your name?' I then asked her.

She, like the others, looked at the Sister for permission to speak.

'That's our Lucille,' said the Sister. 'Aren't you, Lucille?'

'That's a nice name,' I said. 'And what's your second name?'

'Kells,' she said, all shy. 'Lucille Kells.'

Now that I knew what they'd renamed her, I could let the years roll by and see what happened. Fifteen years went by before I went looking for her again. Only now I didn't know where she was.

A pretty secretive world, the orphanage system. Tracing kids isn't easy. I could break into the Health Board's office and go through their computers till her name came up. The same for adoption placement agencies. Maybe she'd later been adopted. Break into

Church computers, those of the Registrar of Births, Marriages and Deaths. Everything's computers these days. Employ a snoop? I know a few good ones, who could get me any kind of info. Lucille Kells could be registered with credit-card companies, the driving-licence department; have a medical card, store cards. Any number of ways of finding her.

A lot of guys in my position would've kept closer tabs on her through the years – tailed her the day of her release, got to know her by being helpful until, and if, she made a move on Clonkeelin, then taken it from there. All kinds of options. Not me. Why would an apparent stranger go to those lengths? Why risk being seen by the law as the first person to help her on her release then, following the deaths of those she believed were her birth family, the Donavans, leave yourself open to all kinds of suspicion?

What I'm saying is – if it could be proven that I'd taken an interest in Lucille, it would form a link. Fuck that. I'm way too cautious for that. How do you think I've stayed ahead of the law all these years? As far as anybody knew, I did not know Lucille, and she did not know me. And that's how it was gonna stay.

The fact was Lucille was in her early twenties before I tracked her down. A car accident left me with two broken legs and, because the left one'd been broken when I was a kid – Christian Brothers threw me out of an upstairs window – and hadn't been treated properly, the second break wrecked it. Left me with twenty-eight per cent bone density from the shin down, screws, plates, all that, crutches for a couple of years, the limp worse than ever.

Anyway, I'd worked out a long time ago, and this was reinforced as I got older and came across some of the kids I'd grown up with, that the religious – the Crucifix Brigade who brought me up, some of them anyway – had a system for naming dumped kids. I'd met up with a kid called Brag. He found out his real name was Brown. He came from Athenry in County Galway. They'd used the first two letters of his real name 'BR' and added the 'A' from Athenry and the 'G' from Galway and came up with Brag for easy reference. B-R-A-G. Dock: 'DO' being the first two letters of my real name Donavan, 'C' for Clonkeelin, 'K' for Kildare. That's how they'd arrived at Dock. I met another lad who hadn't been able to find out his real name. I knew him as Tom Crew. I told him he'd probably discover that his real name began with 'CR' and that he came from some town beginning with 'E' in a county beginning with 'W'. Waterford or Wexford, or some place like that. That's the way the bastards have you, y'see – running around buying maps to find out where you come from. I'm not saying they did this countrywide, but it did go on a fair bit. Another lad was called Lord. I didn't fancy his chances. Lord, like Kells, is a religious name. Since the religious didn't know where Lucille came from, they'd obviously come up with her name and offered it up in their prayers or some crap like that. Unknowns – those babies who were abandoned without paperwork, as opposed to those whose backgrounds were known – were given names with a religious connotation to them. That's my theory. The nuns probably named her after a ninth-century holy book that was written by some monk, *The Book of Kells*.

Kells is also a very rare name. In the phone books countrywide there are only a few dozen of them. And how many of those would be called Lucille? Dock's the same.

It's not a common name either. Ring up directory inquiries and ask for a Robert Dock – different than asking for a Robert Murphy. To tell you the truth, before I went looking for her, it hit me when I kept seeing all the kids going about with mobiles to their ears. I thought maybe Lucille had come out of that orphanage and settled in the nearest city. So I rang the mobile-phone directory inquiries for Galway. No good. Her name wasn't registered with them. I told them to try Dublin. Kids have a habit of flocking to the capital. There was one Lucille Kells in Dublin. I had a number. But that's all I had.

I gave it a go. 'Lucille Kells?'

'Yes?'

I fed her some crap that added up to 'I have a letter which I have been asked to pass on to you from Connemara. Cellphone gave me your number, but not your address.'

'Number two, Primrose Avenue, Dublin Four.'

'Thanks.'

The easy ways are often the best. I took a spin round to Primrose Avenue to make sure I had the right girl. There she was. The sweater she was wearing covered that port wine stain on her arm, but it was her, right up to that red blemish in her eye. Oddly enough, I rarely saw that arm of hers again. She always seemed to wear long sleeves. Embarrassed by it, I suppose.

I followed her for a while after that, found out she worked in a café, shared her flat with an unemployed girl, Gemma Small, one of the kids from the orphanage, got to know some day-to-day stuff about them.

All I had to do now was let her know who she was – Anne Donavan's daughter.

And the only way to do that was by giving her her birth certificate.

The trouble was, I couldn't just send it to her. It had to look right.

I remembered how some of the kids I grew up with had been treated when they left the home. Sometimes they'd be told who they were, usually by being given letters that had been sent to them over the years by relatives, which had been kept from them. There are so many variations on how kids were treated that I could go on forever telling you about them. The religious, for whatever reason, didn't treat us all with the same consideration. Some kids were given info about them-selves, most weren't. The thing was, it was plausible to be given it. Lucille would know that. So I went back to the orphanage where I'd left her and asked, in passing, about the sister I'd seen Lucille with. 'Oh, she's moved on to such and such a place,' I was told.

'Oh, and what about Sister …? I used to love talking to her … What's this her name was?'

'Sister Joseph?'

'Yeah.' Yeah, m'bollocks.

'Oh, dear Sister Joseph passed away five months ago.'

I was in. It was only a question of posting the cert to Lucille, saying Jo had asked for it to be passed on. It wasn't the first time it'd been done. And Jo wasn't around to call me a liar.

LUCILLE

When I was eighteen I went to Joyce House in Dublin.

'Hello.'

'Hello, what can I do for you?'

'Tell me who I really am please.'

Two years later they'd completed their search. 'Sorry, nothing exists on you prior to your being left on the orphanage steps as a baby.'

'OK, bye now.'

'Bye.'

That pretty much sums it up.

A job in a café paid the bills and because meals were included I was able to put by a little each week while I waited for a place at University College Dublin for a degree in psychology and social studies. I wanted to become a child psychologist. That was how I saw my future and I'd resigned myself to the fact that I would never find my mother.

But then a letter arrived containing my long birth certificate and a note from a Sister Joseph, telling me who I really was: Frances Anne Donavan, daughter of Anne Donavan, Clonkeelin, County Kildare.

The question was how to deal with it. Giving me Anne as a middle name was a good sign of course, but I'd have to remember that Anne Donavan herself hadn't sent me the letter and what that implied. A mother doesn't give up her baby without a very strong reason. Whatever her present circumstances, whether she had a husband and children who didn't know about me, or was unable or unwilling to trace me, I would have to approach her in such a way that she wouldn't see me as someone who would upset the life she had now made for herself.

It required a good long think.

RED DOCK

I now needed to know how Lucille would react to receiving that birth cert. If she went out to Clonkeelin to see who she thought was her mother, I could follow her. But that wouldn't tell me what they'd said to one another. And it wasn't as if I could ask her. I could do the next best thing. I could ask her flatmate, Gemma Small. She'd know. But first I'd have to get to know her and gain her confidence.

By this time, I had pubs and hotels. (Whoever said crime doesn't pay can't have been any good at it.) I'd built up a few over the years, all paid for courtesy of outwitting Chilly Winters. Crime seemed to be the only option for me when I came out of that home. I couldn't think of any other way to get what I really wanted (going to the law wasn't gonna get me it), and I'm not talking about personal wealth. I found villains refreshingly honest. They knew what they were and didn't try to paint themselves as saints. I did the odd bit of work for Charlie Swags, but nothing like I used to. The money for the hotels had mostly come from surveillance work. It was an old scam – catch people with money fucking women on camera. The trick was not to let them know I was behind it, amusing myself. I had two hotels. Small-scale. The odd whore brought in the odd celeb and I made sure they got a room next to the one I use for recording embarrassing goings-on. I even had photographs of Chilly himself in bed with a girl. And her name wasn't Mary. But that's another story.

Anyway, Gemma Small went to the job centre a lot … interviews … back to the centre. Wanted work but didn't seem to be having much luck. So I waltzed in behind her one morning, saw her looking at the vacancies and went up to her.

'Mind if I ask you a question?'

'No.'

'I'm looking for bar staff, and I'm in a hurry. If I put the job through here, they'll take days to find someone.' I'd actually seen a TV programme about employers doing this; apparently it wasn't uncommon. 'What d'you think? It's hard work and long hours. If you're not up to it, say.'

'Where?'

'The Copper Jug. Usual rates. Nick and you'll get my boot up your arse.' A bit of humour goes a long way with kids. 'Graft and I'll bung you the odd few quid extra.'

Big smile. When they start palming their locks and blushing, your bullshit's hitting home. Still, there's a lot of dodgy characters around – a girl has to be on her guard. The cops were warning girls – particularly small-chested ones, for some reason – about some nut the newspapers had nicknamed 'Picasso', who was going around leaving them in serious need of sticking plasters. He'd helped himself to over twenty so far, and now he'd started taking them in pairs.

'Check with yer woman behind the desk, if you like. She'll tell you I'm straight up. I've employed the odd few from here before. If you tell the taxman about the bung, OK by me, but you'll go down in my estimation. Am I tempting you?'

The left lock went into her mouth and got on giggling terms with her tongue. Nice little thing – blonde and fuckable.

'One thing – can you add up?'

'Yeah.'

'Good. Make sure you get your fair whack of the tips.'

Another little giggle. 'When do you want me to start?'

'Right away.'

'Will I be all right like this?'

'Why wouldn't you?' Nice lemon sweater and jeans. Very presentable. 'What's your name?'

'Gemma Small.'

'Red Dock. C'mon.' I'd the motor outside. Still with the Mercs. 'I'll ask you some questions about yourself on the way over. Is that all right? Usual employment stuff for the paperwork.'

'OK.'

'That's not a Dublin accent you've got. Where you from?'

'Galway.'

'Great pub town. Your people still live there?' I knew she had none.

'I was brought up in a home.'

'Oh, you're an orphan?'

'Don't know.'

'Find out. Go to the health board. Listen to me going on. Sorry. It's your own business.'

'The health board are useless.'

'I know.'

She wondered how I knew.

Thinking on my feet here, improvising to keep the topic going. 'A mate of mine called Ted Lyle has a couple of girls working for him in your position. One of them went to a support group.'

News to her. 'A support group?'

'They have them for everything: booze, dope, kids in trouble and kids like you. I'll get Ted Lyle's girls to have a word with you, fill you in.'

'Thanks.'

So far so good. *Red the Revelation.* The health boards are a fucking joke. Kids go to them and get told sweet fuck all sometimes.

I left the conversation like that. I'd only wanted to know how she felt about her background so I could use it as a talking point to learn Lucille's feelings on the subject.

Then I rang Ted Lyle and told him I'd a young girl – 'Pretty little thing, she is' – who'd like a word with one of his. The 'pretty little thing' would make him take a look.

No need to make it any more obvious than that. He'd get around to it. Ted had a room-service angle on the go with hotel porters. Class girls. No tarts in lampshades. Throwing one of them a few quid to get the leg over once a week does me. Fuck all that emotional crap. Sex, then get t'fuck outta there's as far as I go. 'So you can send Sally over on Friday night,' I told Ted. Size ten, hair like a seal's, that was Sally.

I was in the office at the back of the Copper Jug that Friday night. I usually count the takings on a Friday. Gemma was in the bar serving.

'Gemma, c'mere a minute and give us a hand.'

Fra – Fra manages the place for me – gave me a bit of a 'don't keep her long' look. The place was crammed. Tina Turner was belting out 'Steamy Windows' on the jukebox. Seemed appropriate. The upstairs ones'd be steamy when Sally got her kecks off.

'Yes, Red?'

I led her into the office. 'Count that, will you?' There must've been twenty-odd grand on the desk. The sight of it made her eyes ping. The first time anybody'd trusted her, by the look of her.

'I'm expecting company, Gemma. Send her up when she arrives. Sally her name is. She's one of the girls I was telling you about who'd fill you in on those support groups. Have a word with her when she's finished.'

I left her to it. Sally arrived and Gemma sent her up. I fucked Sally then sent her down to tell Gemma to give her two hundred quid. Nice and casual. As if Sally was nothing more than hired help. That's all she was anyway. Then I had a shower and came down.

'How you getting on, Gemma?'

She'd figured out what the two hundred was for but didn't say. Just looked embarrassed. 'OK.'

'Good. Give that to Fra when you're finished. I'm away. See ya.'

That was it. A few Fridays came and went. Nice girls with them. Gemma had to know that she herself, being young and attractive, was not of particular interest to me as far as it came to fucking her – that I paid for girls when I wanted them and wasn't into making passes. Detached.

I let this situation between me and Gemma build up over the weeks. I say 'situation'. I won't use the word 'relationship'. It's not a word I feel comfortable with. I haven't felt anything for anyone since Sean. Gemma was to be used, nothing more. How she felt about me, I neither knew nor cared. Distance. I always keep my distance from people. I didn't want my emotions getting in the way of what I was about.

The thing was, Gemma went to a couple of Charlie Swags's nightclubs on weekends and got into Sally's company. Which meant she got into Ted Lyle's. All you have to do is look at Ted to know what he's thinking. When you see him coming all suave – if jewellers displayed their wares on pimps, Ted'd be a walking model for them – Mr 'No Problem' – you know he's making a move. He was looking at Gemma and seeing pound signs. And if he didn't tell Sally to tell Gemma that she could see them too, if she came and worked for him, he wasn't the greedy fucker I knew him to be. Oh he'd take it nice and easy. Everything aimed at making Gemma feel comfortable with Sally's way of earning a living. A lot of girls you can just put it to them straight. Tell them they've got the goods and do they want to get the best returns from them? Other girls would take it as an insult of course. But by allowing a girl to gradually get used to the idea that someone like Sally was making plenty, doing all right for herself, being looked after, no violence, all that, if a girl is of a mind, it slowly begins to seep in that it's just a good way to make money. Five or six punters a night, five or six hundred in their pockets a night. The important thing is not to rush it. I'm telling you stuff you probably already know here. If you don't, fuck knows where you've been living.

The following Friday night, Gemma's counting the money. She's expecting, as usual, a girl to turn up for me to fuck. I hadn't ordered one, but I didn't tell Gemma that. I didn't say a word – just let her think I had. I went upstairs, came down a half-hour later.

'No sign of one of Ted Lyle's, Gemma?' Straight face. Always keep a straight face. Gemma had to have the impression I dealt with girls simply on a business level. I paid bar staff for a service; I paid girls for a service.

'No,' she said. No red face now. She'd become used to it.

'Fuck it.' I sat down at the desk beside her. 'I hate people screwing up my routine.'

'I know.'

I read nothing into that. I'd been let down. Nothing serious. No big deal. But Gemma, I was sure, liked the honesty of my situation, the way I acted, the straightforwardness of it all. No hassle. A 'service' hadn't turned up, that's all. It was important that Gemma felt that although my set-up might be unusual to many, it was normal to me. I could get girls on a phone call. Gemma, therefore, had to see herself as just another girl.

'I'm gonna ask you a question here, Gemma. Say yes or no. It's no big deal to me either way. I can easily ring Ted Lyle and tell him to get his finger out.'

She sensed what was coming. Her face went red and a gulp was on the way. 'What is it?' came out with a 'Fuck me, what's he gonna ask me?' attached to it.

'I want to fuck you.' Unorthodox? Not to me. Depends what you're used to. She knew it was just business. But there was a risk. I didn't want to frighten her off.

Timid little thing. I could see the nerves jumping in her. She took her time. I used it against her.

'No problem,' I said, with no hint of anything in my voice approaching bad feelings – I'd taken her silence as a no, but fuck it, so what?

'All right,' came out. A letter at a time, it sounded like. Maybe she felt something for me; maybe she felt I'd been let down. Kids of her age look up to people who've been good to them. Don't like to feel they've let them down.

'Sure?'

'Yes.' It croaked out. She cleared her throat. 'Yes.'

'OK. Come on. Here.' I handed her two hundred. 'Makes no odds to me who gets this.'

Up we went.

I keep the bedroom nice. I rarely sleep in it. The bar staff know why I use it. No doubt the other waitresses and Gemma had talked about me amongst themselves, how I never hit on staff (and some of them were more than fuckable), how I kept it all on a detached business footing. Maybe Gemma felt a little special. I neither knew nor cared. She'd bunged the money into her back pocket anyway.

I peeled off and sat up on the bed. She went to lie next to me.

'Get the gear off, Gemma.'

Took her aback, that one. Perhaps she thought this would be a necking session to begin with, or a touch of lovemaking foreplay. She might've been into love-making. I fuck – that's it. She stood back up, looking nervous. The light was low. I wanted to see the goods. I'd a reason. Not the turn-on one – another one.

Gemma had no tits. She wore thick jumpers trying to hide it. Why? Self-conscious probably. You know what young girls are like, always worrying about how they look. If they're well stacked, they think they're top heavy; if they've nice tits, they think their arse is too big, or their hair's … I dunno, something wrong with it anyway. Gemma was built like a kid. Smaller than I usually go for, but she was nice all the same.

I ignored the way the shyness was getting to her.

'You've a nice figure, Gemma,' I told her, just to

make her feel better. Helped get rid of her inadequate look anyway. Fuck knows what she was worried about. Some men go in for kid-like girls.

'OK – I like a blowjob then a fuck. OK?'

Shoulda seen her face. The gulp came quicker this time.

I was sitting up. She knelt on the bed and gave me a blowjob. Then I fucked her. I won't describe it. I'm sure you know what a blowjob and a fuck are like. If not, ring Ted Lyle. And if you want to find out what other kinds of sex are like, he's your man too.

She even cuddled into my chest afterwards. No pro ever did that before. I didn't fancy the cuddle.

'OK, Gemma,' I said. 'I have to be going.'

'Did you like it?' she asked. Jesus, I dunno. Talk about insecure kids.

'Of course. You're nice. I have a thing for girls who shave between their legs though, but other than that, fine.'

Her reaction to that would tell me something in the weeks to come.

'Next Friday night? OK by you?'

She nodded. Went red again too. It was my way of proving I'd meant what I said. That she was worth the money.

Now the following Friday, I got what I'd hoped for. I could tell by the way she'd been acting all week that the fuck was between us. I doubt she'd mentioned it to the others. Maybe she did. But there was something in her shy little smile when she passed me or caught my glance. Kids' stuff.

And when I took her up to the bedroom to repeat the exercise, there it was. The jeans came off. She was watching for my response. The pants came down. It was comical. Sweet, some might say. Not me. Though I let on I was pleased. She stood before me, her skin as pink as a newborn. And the blonde hair had gone. She'd shaved it for me. The smile of embarrassment and of waiting for my reaction said it all.

I pulled her over and kissed her. She read affection or love or some such shit in it. It wasn't there. Just manipulation.

OK, you're probably wondering what all this is leading up to. How would Gemma having electrolysis tell me how Lucille had reacted to that birth certificate?

Well, it's like this: there's probably a fancy word in the dictionary for people like me, and I don't know what it is, but what I do know is that I seem to have a way of adapting other people's circumstances to help my own.

Me and Charlie Swags play poker every Sunday night. Have done for years. It's not one of these schools like you see sometimes where you need a big wad to get in. The money is big, but it's incidental. Me and Charlie and a few lads going back a lot of years get together and that's it. No one else.

He was telling me there a while back about a guy called Drake who owned a garage with land attached to it near the city centre, enough land to build a night-club on. Charlie wasn't interested in the garage. He was gonna sell that bit off. The price had been agreed and

Charlie'd had plans drawn up and all that. Then Drake started fucking about, wanting more money. Charlie was fed up with the cunt.

So while all this business with Gemma was going on, what Charlie was saying was beginning to tie in with it. How and why would be too difficult to go into now. Call it instinct, a sense of what might happen – it's up to you. But with me, both Gemma's and Charlie's situations were coming together. I was starting to look at them as a likely opportunity.

What I did was I started avoiding the Copper Jug on a Friday night. Gemma would read stuff into it, I figured, that maybe I was avoiding her. I wasn't, yet I was. I just wanted to see how it played out. I knew that by spending Fridays in The Minstrel, one of my two hotels, Sally would – not would, *might* – tell Gemma that I'd got Ted Lyle to send girls over there instead. Which I did. Fra might tell Gemma that I sometimes spent Fridays in my other places. I went to the Jug Monday afternoons, or something like that, instead.

I popped in one such afternoon and there she was, with a big smile on her face, glad to see me. 'Red, how's it going?' and all that.

I acted like nothing was untoward. 'Gemma, how's it going?' There was something different about her though. Ted Lyle hit me with it weeks later, and I told him he was imagining things. Anyway, I was in the office when she came in for a new till roll.

'I meant to ask you, Gemma.'

'Yes?' sprang out of her like a big exclamation mark, which she checked, realising she was coming across a bit eager. A flattened down version of 'Yes?' followed.

'How'd you get on with that support group? Any luck?'

She lit up, yet looked nervous at the same time. 'I found out who my mother is.'

'You're kidding?'

'No. Honest.'

I didn't care. I was hoping for news of what Lucille was up to.

'Sit down,' I said, 'and tell me all about it. If you *want* to now. I don't want you to think I'm prying. Just interested, hoping things are working out for you.'

'Sure if it hadn't been for you, Red, I might never have found out.'

'Don't be daft.' I pulled up a chair. We were both sitting on what you might call the visitor's side of the desk. 'Hang on a minute and I'll close this door,' I said, as if we were in for a heart-to-heart. 'Don't want everybody hearing your business.'

I won't say she lit up again from then on in, but everything about her definitely sparkled. Her nice blonde tit-length hair was making me feel like having another poke at her. I say blonde, but it was more white-blonde than the yellow kind. Nice eyebrows. Great mouth. She leaned forward in her chair a lot, emphasising.

'I'm going to write my mother a letter,' she told me. 'She lives in Allens, County Longford.'

'What's her name?'

'Angela Reading.'

The Connemara orphanage must've used a different system than the Dublin one I was in.

'Her name was Smart when she had me.'

Ah, same system. As Smart starts with 'SM', the 'AL' was for Allens with the final 'L' for Longford. That's how they'd come up with 'Small'. If I'd thought about it long enough I'd probably have come up with it myself, plus a few more possibilities.

'The trouble is, Red, I don't know what to say to her.'

'Why not just say you've been thinking about her and would like to have a chat? That you'd travel up – in case she might find it difficult to get away, y'know, save her maybe making up yarns to her family. One meeting. Then take it from there. Tell her you're working and taking good care of yourself – mothers like to hear stuff like that – and it'll also tell her that you won't be a burden to her; just in case she'd be worried. You don't know her circumstances. Make it sound like you're your own girl. That's how I'd run with it. That you're initially hoping to strike up a no-strings friendship.'

'Oh, Red, you're so understanding.'

'Just older than you, Gemma. Age gives you a common-sense perspective, that's all. Want me to type it up for you? Longhand's OK, but it might strike of intimacy. Just an idea.'

'Oh, would you?'

'Sure.' I pulled the keypad and the monitor round. 'Fire away.' I then came across as if I'd been acting the know-all. 'Listen to me. This is your private business. What right have I to be taken into your confidence like this? I wasn't thinking, Gemma, I'm sorry. Why don't you write what your flatmate wrote to hers? What's her name again?'

'Lucille. But no, listen – I want you to write it. Your idea's good. Anyway, Lucille's not writing to her mother.'

'Oh?'

'She doesn't look at it the same as me.'

Fuck it. Lucille wasn't going to contact Anne Donavan. That's all I could think of as I typed Gemma's letter. That's the trouble with this game: you can never predict how it'll turn out. Some kids want fuck all to do with the person who gave them up. I'd had it in mind that she'd contact Anne, who'd of course deny she was her mother. It wouldn't matter. She wouldn't be the first to deny she'd given her kid into care. Lucille wouldn't believe her. Official documents, birth certificates, don't lie. Lucille would come away believing she'd been rejected all over again, which, it could be argued, would add to her sense of grievance. For the revenge angle I was working on, y'see, I needed her to confront her mother.

There was nothing else for it. I'd have to force Lucille to go out to Clonkeelin, and to do that I'd have to up the emotional pressure on her.

Some of the kids I'd grown up with had sought out their birth mothers for no other reason than the fact that they had no one else in the world. They came out of the home and were alone. Adopted kids are different in that sense. They have their adoptive families. They're part of something. That's why some of them never trace their roots, I believe. They're emotionally shored up.

In that sense, Lucille had someone: Gemma. They were close. Without Gemma, Lucille would be alone. Bereaved, she might then begin taking steps into her past.

'You'll have to sign this.'

'OK. What do you think I should write?'

'How about "Love, Gemma"?'

'OK.'

'"Love, Gemma" it is.'

And that's what she signed, after reading it four or five times, full of trepidation: longed to send it but was full of uncertainty, all that.

I told her I was going to the post office later, and that I'd mail it for her.

But I'd no intention of doing that. Angela Reading would never see it. Therefore she'd never reply to it. *I* was gonna do that. And I was gonna do it in such a way that when Gemma read it, she'd feel her mother had rejected her all over again. If Gemma had given any indication that Lucille had gone to Clonkeelin, what happened next wouldn't have happened. There'd have been no need for it.

LUCILLE

Doctor Nolan looked to be in his early thirties, too young to have been my mother's doctor when I was born, and had been practising in Clonkeelin for just under three years. When I showed him my birth certificate and explained why I had come he agreed to tell me what he could.

'What are her circumstances? Is she married for instance?'

'No.'

'Divorced?'

'Not that I know of.'

'Does she have any children?'

'No.'

'Does she work in the village?'

'She runs an equestrian business. The Donavan Riding Stables.'

'Does she live alone?'

'No, with her father. His two sisters still live in the old family cottage; it's at the entrance to the farm.'

'How do you think my return might affect her?'

'In a situation like this, if the person involved is elderly or of a nervous disposition, I would suggest that I mediate. I would write her a letter and inform you of her response. Anne is neither of those. Have you considered writing to her?'

I had. But sending a letter's a bit like sending a résumé: it doesn't always lead to an interview.

My friend Gemma was facing the same situation. Only she had written her mother a letter. She'd been talking about it then had it posted before telling me, which meant I couldn't tell her about seeing Doctor Nolan. It only would have upset her to think she hadn't thought to give her mother the same consideration. Besides, it probably wasn't important. After all, I'd imagined Anne Donavan married with kids and possibly not in the best of health and Doctor Nolan had just told me otherwise.

The equestrian business made it possible to approach her on that level. So I bought jodhpurs, boots, waxed jacket, gloves and hat, new seat covers for my Fiesta and gave it a good polish. Then I fixed my hair in plaits and drove in past the cottage where my two great-aunts lived and up the long rambling drive to the main house. It couldn't be seen from the road. It lay in a glade, about half a mile in. A big dormer bungalow with an entrance porch and a conservatory on the end facing the paddocks.

I parked in the stable yard and walked across to an outdoor arena where a man was jumping a horse. He nodded as he rode past. He bore no resemblance to me; resemblance was what I was looking out for. I put him in his late fifties, dark hair as short as eyelashes and stocky.

Then I heard a voice say 'Can I help you?' and I turned around and saw a woman in her late thirties walking towards me.

'Yes, I've a ... come for riding lessons.'

'Now?'

'Only if it's convenient.'

'Of course.'

'Lucille Kells.'

'Nice to meet you, Lucille. Anne Donavan.'

It was her.

Though again I saw no resemblance. She was pretty but did not look at all like me. Perhaps I favoured my father. Her hair was long, like mine, and she wore it in a middle parting, the way I often do, but she was much fairer.

I'd known girls over the years who'd been afraid to meet their mothers. They'd traced them, gone up to them in the street as strangers and asked for directions, just to see if they would detect anything of themselves in them – a set of the jaw, a glint in the eyes – only to be told which way to go. This was very much the same. Still, it was strange standing there with her not knowing who I was.

'Have you ever ridden before, Lucille?'

'No.'

'Come on then, we'll get you going.'

'Are you going to teach me?'

'Of course. If that's all right?'

'Yes. Perfect.'

I hadn't thought of her teaching me personally. I thought she'd have staff. I was delighted though – it would give me a chance to get to know her quicker.

We went over to the stables, where she saddled two horses.

'Now just put your foot in the stirrup and up you go.'

And up I went. Then she showed me how to hold the reins. 'Between your second and third fingers. That's it. Grand.' Big smile. 'And do your jacket up, Lucille, there's a twist in the air.'

She was very friendly and informal. I liked her.

She got up on her horse. Marty she called it. He was much bigger than mine, which was white and called Flo.

'We use Flo for all our beginners. She'll just follow me. I stop, she stops. She likes stopping.'

'OK.'

We went along a trekking lane and across fields to a river.

'Today's just to help you find your seat. Once you get the feel of the saddle, I'll try you out in the lunging arena, lunge you in a circle, going from trot to canter.'

'Have you always lived here?'

'Yes.'

'And is this what you do every day?'

'No. Most of our business comes from tourists. They start off from here with a saddlebag, trek across country to a guest house, stop over then do the same the following day. The routes are all worked out for them on a map. We breed as well, though that's more of a hobby. That was my mare in the first stable. She's a prizewinner. She's due in a few months. To Palermo. The stallion my father was jumping.'

That's how I found out he was my grandfather.

I met him when we got back. The phone in the house was ringing, and while Anne went to answer it I walked around to the lunging arena where he was grooming Palermo. He asked if I'd enjoyed my ride. I said I had. He didn't recognise me though. He didn't give that impression. Odd, really. I was beginning to wonder if I had the right Donavans.

And that's about it. Just horse talk on an hour's trekking. They said it was nice to meet me, and off they went to see about the village show. Anne had mentioned it earlier. They were on the committee. I'd already decided to go to it. Anne had said that her two aunts would be there. I wanted to have a look at them too for family resemblances. Edna and Amy they were called.

I was glad I'd gone about it the way I had. It narrowed things down. By meeting Anne as a stranger, I could gradually get to know her, prove that I was my own person, who would not hurt her in any way. Children were given up in Ireland because of the Church: unmarried mothers bringing shame on their families, reasons I won't go into. But force was often used and enormous emotional pressure exerted. The choice had probably been taken out of Anne's hands. Whatever the reason, those days were gone. I was just a girl who didn't want her mother rejecting her again.

By taking more lessons over the coming weeks, then renting a holiday home for a week, living close by, seeing Anne every day, she might come to look upon me as a friend. Then I'd tell her who I really was.

RED DOCK

I was in the Copper Jug having a pint at the bar when I called Gemma over and handed her a pen and paper. 'Write this down then run it through the word processor for me, will you? To Marshal and Cochrane. They're drink distributors; you'll find their address in the book.'

'OK.'

'"Dear sir." New line. "I've had enough. I'm not taking any more. It's not worth the hassle. Nothing's working out."'

As suicide notes go, it wasn't the best. I couldn't be too obvious about it. I couldn't start saying stuff like 'I've had enough of this "life".' She'd have thought I wasn't right in the head. As it was, she was wondering what it was all about. It was in her handwriting – that was the main thing.

'They're messing me about with corked wine. One look at that and they'll be on the phone begging to keep my custom. Might get a price reduction. Print it out and stick it in an envelope.'

I stayed away from the Jug after that, kept in touch with Fra by phone, had a casual drink with Ted Lyle and just dropped it into the conversation that I thought he'd have added Gemma to his list.

'You surprise me, Ted. I thought you'd've been in there.'

'Some girls do, some girls don't, Red.'

'That surprises me too, Ted.'

He was bound to know I'd paid Gemma for it a few times. How, I don't know. The bar staff might have talked. Gemma could've told Sally and it got back to Ted. Not important. He knew. What he said proved it to me.

'You're a fucking eejit, Red. She went with you because she's in love with you. Not for money.'

I laughed it off. 'Fuck away off, Ted. And you're supposed to know women.'

To be honest, I didn't think I'd let her get that close to me. I can't bear the thought of anyone having those kind of feelings for me. 'In love?' Fuck that. I can't explain why intimacy hits me like vomit – it just does. The thought of someone 'wanting' me, Jesus. And 'in love'? What a corny way to put it. Not at all like Ted. Usually it's 'she fancies you' or some shit like that. Less sting in it.

'Wise up, Ted, for fuck's sake. Put one of your big-shot weekends together, get Sally to invite Gemma on the quiet, liquor her up. Let her find a grand in her pocket next morning. That'll put you straight.'

'What do you care whether she works for me or not,

Red? I've never known you to take this interest before. Anybody'd think she got to you.'

'Got to me, my bollocks. Swagsy has a difficulty coming up. She'll do nicely for it.'

If Ted didn't run with a nudge like that, he wasn't the villain I knew him to be. I didn't need to explain it to him. The remark automatically told him that a 'difficulty' that included Charlie Swags using one of his girls meant he'd be in for a slice. And a slice from Charlie was like a whole vanload from somebody else. He'd run with it all right.

How he'd do it was his own affair. My guess was he'd get Sally to hit her where it would do most damage – her mother. Sally *was* fond of the needle. I wouldn't say she'd more track marks on her arms than a hillwalking map, but she'd a £300-a-day habit and Ted kept her in the best of clients to pay for it.

'Wouldn't you want your mother to see how well you're doing? See what you've made of yourself? Nice car, real money in the bank,' no doubt came into the leverage. I do know that Lyle finished it off by telling Gemma he was short of girls Friday nights – that I was getting fed up with his regulars. She could fill in. He figured that because I saw whoring as nothing to get excited about, she wouldn't think I'd be bothered by her doing it and turn my back on her. She wanted to be near me, he reckoned, and would do whatever it took.

My own guess is she went with it because of her mother. Fuck all to do with me. I wasn't the attraction.

52

Read it any way you like. It happened. That's all I know or give a bollocks about.

I'm in The Minstrel and in walks Gemma. I take her upstairs and act no differently than before. She comes at me a lot closer, with the sighs of emotion and all that crap, and when she leaves, she's looking back at me, as if she doesn't wanna go, as if she wants to stay only with me, that she'll do it because I'm part of the package. Did you ever hear such a pile of shit in all your life? 'Love' – Jesus, no thanks. The last thing she said to me was: 'See you next week, Red?' I gave her a smile to keep her going. That was it. Thank fuck for Charlie, that's all I can say. This stuff with Gemma was stirring shit in me that I didn't want stirring.

By this time, things had moved on as far as what Charlie Swags had said to me was concerned. My reading of him turned out to be right. I knew a bit more about this than I said earlier. And it all added up to Charlie walking in looking like things had just taken a turn for the worse. And he walked into The Minstrel.

Now knowing Charlie as I do, I know his moods – whether he's pissed off because things haven't gone as planned or if there's something personal in it. And that's what this had come down to.

Drake – that fucker who owned the garage I was telling you about – had decided not to sell, and he was putting it about that he'd made a fool out of the 'Great' Charlie Swags. Which was a load of bollocks. It was simply a deal that had fallen through and Charlie would've seen it like that if Drake hadn't gone mouthing off. Since Charlie was nodding towards the table in the corner, where we got down to the bones of it, it was more than obvious that as he was running it by me, he was looking for something with an edge to it that'd make Drake sell.

So I sat back, gave it some thought, downed a whiskey, nodded to the barman for another round – including a swig for Charlie's two heavies on their high stools – waited till it was brought over, Charlie tipping away at Irish Mist ...

'Drake married, Charlie?'

'He is.'

'Other women?'

'We're all fond of a bit of skirt, Red.'

'Kids?'

'Daughter.'

'How old?'

'Fuck knows. Eleven, twelve ...'

'Hit him there.'

'With what?'

'What do men fear above all other things when it comes to sex, Charlie?'

'Not being able to get it up any more?'

'What else?'

'Ah ...'

Charlie never sees the angles. Even at this stage, when he'd become like one of those guys you read about in the Sundays – 'Crime Boss Guilty of All Sorts of Crap' – he still never sees the angles. Not that he'd ever been in the Sundays, though Chilly Winters had been refusing promotion for years trying to put him in them. Winters was still carrying a grudge over his daughter. He'd found out after she was taken that Charlie was behind it. And Winters knows, more so then than now, that where Charlie went, I went. He blames me too. No proof though. You'd think he'd wise up. In order to beat us, he has to catch us. If he doesn't catch us, that's a reflection on his abilities, a failing on his side. He should look at it like that.

'Y'know that new girl Ted Lyle has working for him, Charlie? She was at a hen party one night in the Carmine Club, wore a dress no bigger than a pillowcase. Long blonde hair, no tits, small enough to go down on a guy standing up; very young looking. Gemma Small.'

'Didn't she used to work for you?'

He'd had his eye on her. Charlie likes them young. 'She's into electrolysis.'

'What's that – some kinda vibrator?'

'No muff.'

'So?'

'Scams are about perception, Charlie. What people *perceive* to be the truth, not the truth itself. Set her up as a tourist in that hotel you said Drake drinks in. Nice and easy does it; she's not to rush. See what happens. Maybe he'll bite, maybe he won't. If he does, it's up to her room with a hidden camera on the go. I'll set it up, all part of the service.' I had surveillance gear, the kind top-notch private investigators use, with built-in phones, microphones, speakers, 'always-on' broadband access, VCR jacks, camera lenses the size of tie pins, the works. I call them surveillance 'laptops', mainly because they're portable, but they're much more than the ones you'd buy in the shops and about twice the size. 'If my guess is right, a little thing like Gemma without the pubic hair will come across on screen as a minor. Send Drake a copy, then ring him up and reduce your offer. When he scoffs, ask him what kind of videos his daughter and her schoolmates like to watch. That'll tell him you're the one who sent it.'

The kid element gave it the edge he was looking for.

'God bless you, Red.'

'No problem.'

'How the fuck do you come up with these scams so fast?'

'You know me, Charlie – always like to have one ready in case of a quick getaway. I'm also a genius.'

Genius, my bollocks. I'm no smarter than the next guy. I just take everything from experience. When I was a kid, I saw two lads with a Christian Brother. They were both about the same age, but one had pubic hair and the other one didn't. The one without it looked a lot more like a minor because of it. That was probably my first lesson on how things look based on how you present them. If you'd shaved the lad with it, he too would've looked like a minor. Your basic everyday logic. That's the lesson I took from it anyway. When I saw Gemma, it came back to me.

I saw the upshot of this, incidentally, when Ted Lyle'd recorded it onto one of my surveillance laptops.

Gemma had a doll's mouth. When she went down on Drake, her lips had a job getting round it. Brought back memories. If I hadn't known better, I'd have said she was only coming into her teens. But I knew her – Drake's wife wouldn't. She'd have seen him fucking what looked like a kid. Then Drake went and got hit by a car and ended up in hospital, and Charlie put that part of it on hold till he was up and about.

Of course, the extra angle was that while we were waiting for Drake to hit on Gemma, others would hit on her. Top hotel, leave the camera rolling, in the hope she goes down on a top cop or a politician. Or maybe a judge. Nothing like having His Honour in your pocket if the bastard happens to be looking down on you at the time with his wig on. This is the sort of stuff I told you I dabbled in from time to time, when girls brought celebrities back to my hotels. Most of the videos I'd never used. Kept them for my own private collection in case they ever came in handy.

Then there was the money angle. She was bound to pick up businessmen. We could see if they were worth hitting on or not. What could be easier? Clean the cunts for every penny they had; get as much out of a scam as you can.

Women were another angle. If one picked up Gemma, a woman fucking her would give it another extra. All kinds of offshoots. Oddly enough, though I didn't know it at the time, Gemma swung both ways. She had a couple of girlfriends round the clubs.

Anyway, all scams have to end. You can only milk

them for so long. And when they're finished, the girl involved has to go. That's why I'd nudged Gemma into this.

So I sat down and wrote Gemma a letter. She would think it had come from her mother, in response to the one I'd typed for her but never posted. I can't even remember what bullshit I wrote. Something like:

Dear Gemma,

I'm sorry for taking so long to reply to your letter. But as much as I wish things were different, they are what they are ... My family are unaware of my past ... I wish you all the best in life.

Love Angela

The usual 'fuck-off' letter mothers like Gemma's send.

It was to tie in with that suicide angle I was telling you about. The suicide was weak, I grant you that. I hadn't had enough time to work on it. The law'd find Gemma's body on the pavement outside a high-rise, her 'mother's' letter and the one I'd dictated to the drink company in her pocket, pointing to her having jumped because she couldn't live with Angela rejecting her twice. I'd cut the 'Dear Sir' bit off the one Gemma'd handwritten for me. Anyway, that's the way it was supposed to work out. The law would suspect Charlie was behind it, but the suicide note would colour it and keep the pressure off him. He'd expect me to have an angle like that working for us.

I'd driven the sixty miles into Allens, County Longford to mail the letter so it would have the right postmark on it. Gemma would have a read of it the following day then be seen to have bowed out that night. Up the emotional pressure on Lucille, all that. That's how I was seeing it. But I wasn't the only one with designs on Gemma.

Let me put that another way: someone else was intent on *having* designs on her. And when I say designs I mean designs. Literally. And it led to me getting the goods on one of the best killers this town had ever known.

Even I hadn't planned on this one.

PICASSO

Everything was going along superbly, just as I'd planned. And then complacency set in. I'm lucky to be at liberty. Very lucky indeed. Complacency will not set in again. I can assure you of that.

The first error came in the form of two young ladies called Lisa Shine and Jackie Hay.

It had occurred to me that, rather than painting my models from the photographs I'd taken of them, I would instead bring them home and paint at my leisure. After all, did da Vinci paint the *Mona Lisa* from a Kodak, or Sargent *Madam X*? No, they had real-life models. Like them, I too would one day hang in the great galleries of the world. Each portrait would bear the model's own handprint to authenticate its provenance. The world would know me as 'Hockler', and not by the ridiculous sobriquet the press had attached to me. Picasso! Hah! Why would one such as I need the name of another when my talent will one day stand on its own merits? Cornelius Hockler! Ultimately I would send my portraits to every major gallery, and the name Hockler would eventually be every bit as well known as the great masters.

Hah! What absolute drivel. Great masters indeed. If Michelangelo had been born in a hut in the Gobi Desert and had painted the ceiling of the local mosque, instead of the Sistine Chapel, no one would have ever heard of him. Mine is a mediocre talent – like many hanging in the art galleries of the world. What is talent? Often it is only one's ability to be in the right place at the right time. You will observe that I have not said one's 'good fortune' to be in the right place at the right time, which, of course, does apply in certain cases. An artist with a sense for business can discern opportunities using his wit, charm, presentability, his personal allure, his allusiveness perhaps, his articulateness, his ability to endear and elevate himself through colour-blind benefactors, who wouldn't know one end of a brush from an ear pick. Prominent critics authenticate long-lost works, then a forger steps forward and exposes them for what they are – something he knocked out for a laugh. Pompous fools incapable of aiming a stick of charcoal. Yet they judge those who can do far more and, in so doing, ruin their careers. In short: circumstances, serendipity, better publicists, create 'great artists' often much more than their issue. I refer to my work as my issue. They are my babies – all motherless.

In my case, my work will be hailed for its subject matter and its ability to sell tickets. Its notoriety will sustain its appeal. The art world is a sham in which art lovers will come to recognise my paintings in an instant.

61

To date I had painted some, oh, twenty-or so models. I really do not recall the total number. Only eleven singles were of a sufficient standard to warrant exhibiting. The others had not turned out as I had hoped. The bosoms, you understand. Their texture and skin tone cannot be ascertained until clothing has been removed, venal fluids drained and flesh left to settle. Hence their ultimate rejection. No matter; mustn't complain.

I had begun my clandestine career with the notion of formulating a sequence of portraits, each representing the seasons. Then I changed this to months. One portrait representing each of the twelve.

In the UK and the United States, at least, the carnation is the January flower, the primrose February, violet March, daisy April, lily of the valley May, rose June, water lily July, poppy August, morning glory September, calendula October and chrysanthemum November. These portraits I had completed, each depicting a flower, plus something from the Greek, Medusa being a particularly difficult one to encapsulate. I had added the Greek connotation, plus a little something from my own past, to satisfy the pretensions of the art Establishment. Art scholars and critics give more credence to mythology. It allows them to appear erudite. 'Ah, yes,' they would postulate, 'Hockler clearly substituted fingers for snakes to …' I don't know. Whatever they come up with, it will be pure supposition. And wrong. I had not the slightest reason in the world for supplanting snakes, other than to give them something to muse over. I used fingers because I had no snakes. It was that simple.

Alas, I had yet to find a suitable model to complete my collection. Although I had a model in mind – for narcissus, the December flower.

Together these twelve works of art would be known as the 'Hockler Women in Bloom Collection'. I had initially considered the 'Hockler Blooming Women Collection' as a title but, after many sleepless nights of cogitation, settled for the former.

As to why it had occurred to me to bring my models home, well, I simply became fed up with lurking in the shadows until the first suitable female happened by. To photograph under such circumstances is an absolute pain. One has the problem of lighting, weather conditions – on a bad night one risks catching one's death of cold. The times I have had to postpone, you simply would not believe. Weather forecasts are of no help. And, of course, as I have alluded, if a girl is heavily wrapped up, it is impossible to tell what lies beneath her clothing, apropos her overall figure. I cannot work with plump models. A waist is vital. To sketch the stem of the bloom, one must have the curves of the waist to give symmetry. A big belly would look grotesque. And the skin must be taut, not aged and slack. Large breasts, too, are out. One ends up with squashed petals between the cleavage. Small, pert breasts are by far the more desirable.

Thus I went to the bank and arranged a loan to reno-vate my cellar into suitable accommodation. Naturally, I had to carry out the work myself, which involved going to night classes in block laying and welding, to make the doors and the masonry to support them. Finally, when the last block had been mortared, a serving hatch and a peephole fitted in each of the four doors, I loaded Shirley, my dog, into the back of my van, fed her a heavy sedative – nothing harmful, for I would not hurt a defenceless animal – and drove straight to a park that bordered a housing estate on the west of the city – the nocturnal habits of whose residents I had been monitoring for some weeks. I parked in a nearby lay-by used by lorries, from which one could see right along the road in either direction. I enjoyed a little Mozart while waiting. His *Requiem*.

The time was approaching half past ten when I saw the two models I had selected, their Labrador on a leash, crossing at the pedestrian lights, as I had observed them doing on previous evenings. I drove straight in through the park gates, lifted Shirley out and laid her unconscious on the ground, then hunkered over her as they drew near.

'Excuse me,' I began in a very polite and pitiful voice, which, I have found to my advantage, evokes compassion among fellow dog lovers. A hook, if you like.

Their Labrador strained to attend and commenced sniffing Shirley, as dogs are wont to do, in her nether regions.

'What's the matter?' the dark-haired one of the pair asked.

'It's Shirley. She's had an attack of some kind. I'm so worried. Would you mind giving me a hand to lift her inside? I must get her home. Only it's my back, you see. She's too heavy.' I sounded at my wits' end.

'Of course. The poor thing.'

'Oh thank you. You're very kind.'

'Not at all.' She turned to her friend. 'Come on, Lisa. You take her front and I'll take her rear.'

They were so helpful.

My chloroform spray caught them as they stooped. I reached for the two soaked cloths I had prepared moments in advance and pinned their heads back against my chest until they lost consciousness, then gently lifted them, one at a time, into the back, for I did not wish their skin to be bruised. Then I put Shirley in behind them and was gone, their Labrador chasing after the van.

In my cellar, I placed Jackie Hay in room number one, and Lisa Shine in number two, searched their pockets for keys and went to their apartment.

I confess that my career has occasionally forced me to appropriate where and when I can. The cost, you understand – van expenses, materials and so forth. I'm not quite a penniless artist living in a garret. A small trust set up by my father provides a modest monthly income, though not nearly enough. He also left me his surgical instruments, which I use to assist me in my work, and this house, which he himself had inherited. He was a surgeon and an anatomist in Berne, where I spent my early childhood. Like most boys, my wish was to follow in my father's footsteps. I showed a keen interest in his work, attended his lectures, dissections. Alas, it was not to be. I became inured to the sight of human flesh post-mortem, but began to be fascinated by it as an art form. Art was fast becoming my passion. I studied in Vienna and Paris. But, as I have already averred, the art world spurns that which it does not understand, only to praise it when others and time have rendered it unique.

'Grotesque,' they said of my work. 'Twisted'. Lesser talents garnered acclaim through subject matter found in a vase or a meadow. They played it safe. Cowards. No originality. Flowers need not be set in a meadow to attract the art-loving public. Other settings can attract artistic acclaim. As does notoriety. The cutting off of van Gogh's ear is as much in the public consciousness as his *Irises*. I was a great disappointment to my father. And so endeth the personal history lesson, excluding reference to one period in my life to which I shall not refer. It was most disagreeable.

I found little in the way of cash in Jackie and Lisa's apartment. I never take personal items, such as jewellery, and of course never televisions or anything of that nature. Selling them on might attract the police. I do however always take home videotapes.

Jackie's and Lisa's were particularly entertaining. I viewed them at home over a bottle of Chablis. The camcorder on a tripod in their bedroom – which I did help myself to (I had it in mind to film their final moments, which I could then study in detail in order to improve my technique) – had indicated that they were lovers. One tape showed them in bed with a third girl, a delicate little creature with blonde hair, sandwiched between them. I watched them for an hour or so and then an idea presented itself, and I decided to do what I had never done before: indulge myself. I compiled two copies of the tapes and addressed one to each of their mothers.

The fact of the matter was that I had selected the two models because I had never before painted a pair, only singles. And I wished for one particular piece, over and above *December*, to crown my collection. I was also anxious that when the finished work was eventually sent to a gallery of my choosing, its existence would be marked by something fresh and original. A unique provenance, as it were. It would not only depict two lovers, it would carry attached to it the story of how their mothers had been involved in its creation. I had a provisional title for it: *Duet*. Artists must name their work.

Then I went downstairs.

In each of their rooms I placed a very large wooden box, then went into room number three and raised a flagstone. The rats came out from below it – the large black variety that grow to eighteen inches, including the tail – up through a chute I'd made and into a hutch. I closed off the chute, emptied the hutch into the box in Jackie's room, repeated the exercise until it contained thirty or so, bolted the lid, then did the same in Lisa's room.

Rats were not my first choice, I feel it necessary to point out. I had initially considered *Dorylinae* as a method of extracting information. *Dorylinae* may be better known to you as army ants: nomadic predators spectacular in their hunting raids. They form a family group, the *Formicidae*, which divides into ten sub-families. Their posterior abdominal stings inject venom which allows a colony to pick a rhinoceros clean in three days. On the march they will eat any living thing too slow to get out of their way. And therein lay my difficulty. My rooms afforded no sanctuary in which a model *could* get out of their way.

You see, and I concede that I have studied this only on a cursory level, though I have also had some experience from quarters that most people would rather not hear of, the art of interrogation appears to lie in applying the most pressure while creating the least pain. I'm referring to my own particular needs: pressure can be damaging emotionally, whereas pain is invariably damaging physically. Too much physical damage and the model's natural beauty becomes scarred and diminished, and death may occur before information is extracted. Counterproductive. Time is also a factor. By allowing the model to witness the painful outcome of non-cooperation, it is not so much the pain itself but the thought of the pain which generates the most fear.

I had had in mind a variation of an old Native American method. Whereas they would bury a victim up to his neck in sand (ambient temperature courtesy of the parching sun), his mouth fixed agape to facilitate the unbroken flow of treacle from an anthill to his oesophagus, then smash the anthill, enabling the little fellows to eat their way along the trail (their advance to be assessed at his leisure) and find within him enough food to do them for the winter, I myself found the ritual to be unsatisfactory for my own particular purposes, the vocal chords being necessary, as it were, to extract information. Far more conducive to start at a person's other end.

By placing a piece of meat on the ground, then allowing a number of ants to feast upon it, the attentive victim would observe that which lay in store should he or she choose to be uncooperative. By then strapping the victim – in this case my two guests – to the floor, legs apart, and pouring treacle, by way of a funnel, in through their aforementioned 'other ends', the ants could then consume the treacle all the way into their insides, which would be subjected to the same fate as the meat. Nature's original pincer movement.

But I forewent this technique. Ants are difficult to control. Not all would follow the treacle. Others would feast on the subjects' skin. Painting them would be less rewarding, particularly if their faces and breasts had been pincered.

Rats, of course, are ultimately and more speedily capable of creating a similar conclusion. Hence my use of the wooden crates. Once locked in, the rats could not get out; though, to the victim, they eventually would. Which engendered a quandary. What, after all my safeguards, if they did get out? I would not be any more celebratory than my models, whom I did not wish to be blemished. This I would overcome by introducing a measure of incentives. I would furnish replacement timbers, hammers and nails. You may feel constrained to point out that by so doing, my guests could avail of an opportunity to bludgeon me to death, or to knock a hole in the wall and make their escape. Do not alarm yourself. I was imminently cognisant of the former; concerning the latter, the walls' cavities were steel lined and the doors of sufficient tenacity to withstand a horde of Olympic hammer throwers. A trifle overstated, that last remark. My apologies to you for my eagerness to allay your concerns.

Suffice it to say that the self-explanatory nature of the incentives would allow my guests to consider the benefits of incrementally frustrating the rats' inexorable foray by shoring their defences. You may question the wisdom of this. Better to expedite matters without the comfort of reinforcements. I concur. Alas, it has been my unfortunate experience to arrive home late only to discover that the weight of the rats lunging against the inner surface of the crate compounded to create its dislodgement. I did not wish to lose a model in that fashion a second time. Besides, the replacement timbers, one each only, were of lighter quality than those used in the crates' construction. They would prolong, not halt.

Having arranged for both Jackie and Lisa to awake to these considerations, I then got a good night's sleep, and the following morning brought them the radio, for their entertainment, then made myself a nice hearty breakfast.

The news was on as I came back down and found them both gazing out through the serving hatches I'd made for their convenience, listening to the broadcaster reporting that, 'Gardai are calling for information on the disappearance of two young women: Jackie Hay, last seen wearing a red skirt and pink sweater, and her flatmate, Lisa Shine, wearing black Lycra leggings and a lemon V-neck jumper, walking their dog towards St James's Park, south Dublin, last night at around half past ten. Both are aged nineteen. And now the sport.'

Sport – how appropriate.

I switched off the radio and presented myself.

'Jackie, Lisa. I am Hockler.'

They eyed me up and down. I'm quite a figure of a man, you know. Six foot six and not an ounce of fat.

'Please, Mr Hockler—'

'Not "Mr", Lisa, "Hockler".'

'What do you want with us, Hockler?'

'I want you for my work, Jackie. I'm an artist.'

'Please, plea-ease, I've got a little baby.'

'Oh have you, Lisa? How old?'

'Eleven months.'

'You must be very proud.' Odd, I hadn't seen a baby in their flat – not as much as a pair of rubber knickers. And her proclivity to sapphism hardly suggested heterosexual issue. Perhaps the prefix 'bi' would better connote than 'hetero'. 'Now, Lisa, time is moving on. I'll show you where I work.'

I unlocked Lisa's door. She retreated and curled up in the corner, hiding her face.

'Would you rather I showed Jackie?'

Her second and third fingers parted, revealing a

recoiling eye, in turn towards myself, the crate then back again. Then in a barely audible whimper, she uttered, 'No.'

The rats were distracting her. They often get excited at such times, in anticipation of being fed.

Jackie, however, appeared less perturbed by them. 'Leave her alone,' she interceded.

'As you wish.' I locked Lisa's door and unlocked Jackie's.

'What – you expect me to follow you? Just like that?'

'Jackie, you did object to my taking Lisa.'

She hesitated. This was new to me. I had never before had two models (my apologies: prior to renovating, there had been an earlier opportunity which had proved short-lived and therefore unworthy of recounting) and had not expected one to appear to put herself forward in place of the other only to retract. They say that models can be elitist. Clearly this was an example of that. Prima donnas. 'Well?'

Jackie stepped into the corridor, regarding Shirley warily. I had made Shirley crouch at the foot of the steps leading up to the kitchen. She can be intimidating. One cannot have one's models kneeing one's groin and attempting to flee, as one debilitating experience (to which I have just briefly alluded) had taught me.

At moments such as this, I find it most interesting to observe models' eyes and body language. Without exception, wariness, of a different nature to that which she had shown towards Shirley, accompanied Jackie's demeanour. Whereas she had regarded Shirley with alarm, I was treated to a glare, both appraising yet wincing. Her colleague, I suspected, was exhibiting similar apprehension. Alas, it is not a deportment that extends itself to the studio. A pity. I should so like to capture it on canvas.

'This way.' I opened the door to room number four. (I had removed its five incumbents – Shirley's now-grown pups – to room number three. Like the rats, they too, for identical reasons, can become overexcited at the thought of models, once they have outlived their usefulness.)

Shirley came up behind us, growling as we entered.

'She's merely jealous, Jackie,' I explained, 'because I'm holding your hand. She likes me all to herself.' Shirley snarled at her. 'Now, now, Shirley, I've told you about that before. Come along, Jackie.'

I led her in through the internal door and down the steps to my studio. She entered guardedly, the freezer, in particular, as the motor came on, startling her further. The newspapers had reported my having taken what they had referred to as 'physical trophies'. I suspected that Jackie was aware of this disclosure and had now made the connection. She was looking at the freezer the way people do not normally look at freezers, assessing it not as a two-door model with a fridge on the top, but rather in terms of its likely contents. I opened the top door. Strange how such an everyday action in a kitchen can pass unnoticed, yet in a given set of circumstances can engender a heart-stopping reaction.

'Would you care for a soft drink, Jackie?'

She declined or should I say 'jerked' her head repeatedly from side to side. Far too many jerks for one simple 'no'. She had expected the compartment to contain something other than Coca-Cola and pineappleade (the latter a favourite of mine). I did not open the lower door. What she would have seen inside would have put an abrupt halt to my guided tour.

'Now, this is where I work. Not the most luxurious of studios, but I get by. Henceforth I intend to prepare all my models and place them here on this table. As you can see, it has a zinc top, a touch too cold for the purposes of sitting. I have purchased various materials with which to cover it to provide a backdrop: velvet, silk and so forth.'

She herself, of course, would never view the finished work. This too was preying on her mind.

'And when I have finished, I hang my paintings in here.' I showed her through to my private art gallery. She was the first to have ever received a private viewing. 'And here, Jackie: I've reserved this space for you.'

It was quite a commanding space, in the centre of the wall between a portrait of a redheaded model named Clare and a raven-haired model called Katie. Again words failed her, as they would have any female finding herself in this situation. She could hardly take it in.

'Now that wasn't so bad, was it? You can tell Lisa all about it when you get back.'

This was to form a precursor to a little expedient I was contemplating. I had experienced, in my early to mid-teens, that foretaste engenders compliance. More anon.

As I had anticipated, she fainted. I carried her back to her room.

* * *

'Now, I'd like you to tell me about your friends. Girl-friends. You first, Jackie.' The question somewhat betrayed my intentions.

'Why do you want to know?'

'I should like to get to know them.'

'I have no friends.'

'Lisa?'

Lisa was still curled up in the corner, her head on her knees.

'Lisa?'

Nothing. They needed more time. I had surmised as much. Hence my preparations. Though how long they would hold out had yet to be put to the test. The strange thing was that neither had made reference to the rats. They seemed to accept them as part of their predicament, over which remonstrating would hold no sway. Both stayed away from their respective crates, though they were clearly unhappy at their presence, and appeared to cringe more than a little during momentary increases in rustling and so forth, particularly Lisa – but that was the extent of their distraction. This surprised me.

In the case of the rats, as opposed to the ants, experi-ence had taught me that information can be extracted over a period of time, usually no longer than a fortnight, by placing the subject in surroundings such as those I had borrowed good money to engineer, or similar, with no outside contact, a cold floor to sleep on, the rats starving and gnawing at the wood, driven by the smell of what little food the subject was being fed, incessantly squeaking, on and on and on, until the subject begins to hallucinate and then sleepwalks. I then enter, open the box, let the rats loose then leave. The subject then snaps out of it and believes that he or she has let them loose. I then re-enter with a blazing torch, disperse the rats, usher the subject into another room and start again. The subject is then reluctant to go back to sleep in case of a recurrence.

I wasn't quite sure what I would do if none of this worked in respect of Jackie and Lisa. I would clearly have lunatics on my hands. And because lunatics are irrational, irrational thought often has to be applied in dealing with them. I would have to come up with something else. I did not think it would come to that. Moreover, I did not know how to think irrationally.

I tossed an already-dead rat with a knife wound, and a live rat to feed on it, into each of their rooms to exemplify the outcome should the others eat their way through the timber, which, I believe I neglected to add, had been steeped in beef stock to create incentive. The psychological effect of this is advantageous. I left them for thirty-six hours, until the following night, when I returned with a bottle of wine and a glass, pulled up a stool and tried again.

'Tell me about your friends, Jackie.'

'My friends?'

Her spirit had gone. A fortnight had not been necessary after all. The foretaste had contributed towards bringing her acquiescence to fruition. I was so glad. And, of course, anxious to proceed to the studio. 'Yes, girlfriends. Their names, please.'

She came to the door and spoke through the small serving hatch. From the calculated nature of her responses, I knew that she had been assessing her personal relationships. (It reminded me of having been made to go to confession and of being careful to avoid implicating others, especially those who were part of their regime, that is to say the 'religious'. I shall linger on that point only to convey that the seal of the confessional did not safeguard against reprisals. It is unforgivable to raise a subject then refuse to elaborate. Still, such is life sometimes.)

The interrogation book I had read (it was written in an unusual style, incidentally – in a kind of telegraphese) stated: 'Implications of informing on friends or comrades, as seen by subject. Informing by subject would be weighed against the benefits it might bring. Would informing buy subject time? How much time? Enough to escape while information is being verified? Once free, subject can alert comrades, those they have informed on, and thus remove the threat to them which the imparted information might engender. Informing, in that context, means nothing. No one gets hurt. Desperation. The will to live can become paramount. If subject informs, will he or she be looked upon favourably and spared?'

'Who's the third girl with you in the video, Jackie?'

'Gemma Small.'

'Gemma Small? Nice name. Do you think she's pretty?'

'Yes.'

'Who else do you include among your friends?'

'Lucille Kells.'

'And do you think she's pretty?'

A nod. Again, according to the book: 'A nod constitutes less guilt than the spoken word. It makes it seem like the subject isn't naming names.'

'Do you like them?'

'Yes.'

I wondered if that were true. Was she telling me the names of her best friends or of those she disliked? Clearly she did not dislike Gemma. They had shared a bed. Perhaps they had fallen out. I'm sorry, that sounds as if they had fallen out of bed. Perhaps they had *had* a falling out.

'I fancy you are being covetous with the truth, Jackie. You dislike Gemma?'

'Yes.'

I'd suspected as much. In bed, Gemma had shown her back to Jackie in favour of Lisa. Jealousy. Gemma had been in the middle, the enviable of the three positions. Gemma and Lisa had shared the two-way artificial stimulant. The batteries had run out. I recalled Jackie's look of disappointment. Perhaps she had bought the batteries and felt cheated. Perhaps she felt challenged. Gemma was prettier than her.

'Which of you met Gemma first?'

'Me.'

'You were emotionally involved with Lisa at this time?'

'Yes.'

'But contemplating a change?'

She glanced towards Lisa's room, concerned that she should not overhear her response. She nodded.

'Then Lisa met Gemma?'

'Yes.'

'And Lisa contemplated a change?'

'Yes.'

'That's not true,' Lisa sobbed. 'I told you it wasn't true, Jackie.'

'And yet you both loved Gemma, Jackie?'

'Yes.'

'But Gemma departed, leaving each of you to settle for second best – each other – in a relationship you had both intended dissolving.'

'Yes.'

'Ah, the ever-adversarial vicissitudes of the ménage à trois.'

'Gemma didn't live with us.'

'Oh, I see. With whom did she live? Lucille Kells?'

'Yes.'

'But she would not leave her?'

'It wasn't a question of leaving her. Lucille's straight. She and Gemma share a flat, that's all.'

'Where do they work?'

'Gemma works in the Top Towers Hotel.'

'Dublin?'

'Yes. She promotes the hotel, entertains foreign holiday companies' reps. I'm not sure of the details. You'll find her there every night.'

Again I was wondering if she was telling me the truth.

And so it went on, until I knew which nights Gemma Small and Lucille Kells were likely to be vulnerable. Jackie had supplied details I would otherwise have been able to obtain only through long observation. My intention was to avoid the risk associated with picking up models at random, in favour of the relative safety of knowing exactly whom to aim for.

'Thank you, Jackie. Thank you.'

I went upstairs and finished my wine, then brought the portable television, the VCR and my guests' mobile telephones down into the corridor and played their home video.

They came to the serving hatches, surprised by my choice of viewing.

Then I rang Jackie's mother.

'Mrs Hay?'

'Yes?'

'Oh, hello. I'm sure you are anxious to hear from me about your daughter Jackie. Hello. Hello, Mrs Hay, are you there?' I detected a sense of unease, as though Mrs Hay needed breathing salts.

'Yes, I'm here,' she said eventually, light-headedly, as is the way of mothers in her position. 'Please, please don't hurt my daughter. Please don't hurt her.'

'Of course not.' I nodded to Jackie and gave her the

thumbs up, to let her know her mother was concerned for her well-being, but that I had put her fears to rest. 'Tell me, Mrs Hay, what did you think of the videotape I sent you? Jackie is here watching it as we speak.'

I presumed Mrs Hay to be sitting in front of her television set with loved ones, well-wishers, the police expressing their determination and so on.

'What do you think of their performance, Mrs Hay? What part are you at now? We are at the part where Jackie is inserting batteries into one of those – what is it they call them now? She's got such a big smile on her face, as much as to convey: "Look at what I've got for you, Lisa, darling." Lisa looks delighted. I think it's an extra large.'

'Please, please let my daughter go. Please—'

'Let my mother alone!'

'Jackie, please be quiet, if you wouldn't mind. I can't hear your mother. I am so sorry for the interruption, Mrs Hay. You were saying?'

She was too overcome to talk.

I rang Mrs Shine on Lisa's mobile. 'Hello, Mrs Shine, is that you?'

'Yes.'

'Oh good. I'm glad I caught you in. I'm sorry – I forgot to introduce myself. I sent you a videotape. Lisa, I've got your mother on the phone.' Lisa had returned to her corner.

'Please don't harm my daughter.'

'Well, that puts me in a bit of a spot, Mrs Shine. Mrs Hay has asked me not to harm her daughter. And

I agreed, because, well, I had yours. But if I agree to your request, I won't have any daughters left. You do see my position.'

'Leave her alone.'

'Jackie, please stop interrupting. Kindly hold the line, Mrs Shine. Mrs Hay?'

'Yes?'

'Apropos your daughter – a situation has arisen. I've explained my commitment to your good self, and Mrs Shine wishes me to give her the same undertaking. My point is, mothers, I cannot decide which daughter to have first. Mrs Hay, shall I have your daughter first, after all, or would you rather I kept my commitment to you and have her second?'

Shirley starting barking as Jackie screamed, 'Stop torturing my mother, HOCKLER!'

I hung up immediately.

This was the first error I referred to earlier. Had Shirley barked loud enough to drown out my name? Had the police been recording the conversations? Would they analyse the call through enhancing equipment?

Mine was not an Irish name. And few Hocklers lived in Ireland. Would the authorities be at my door before the night was out? You can see why I found the episode distressing.

Complacency, you see. Complacency can be a devil.

LUCILLE

Gemma's letter came. The night I was due to move into the holiday cottage I arrived home from working late to collect my things and found it on the mat. I wouldn't be seeing her for a week, so I took it to the Top Towers Hotel, went up to her room and knocked on the door.

Things weren't well between me and Gemma. I didn't like what she was doing. She didn't want me there.

When she called out, 'Who is it?' and I said, 'It's me,' her voice dropped. 'Lu?'

'Yes.' She opened the door with her back to me. I'd embarrassed her by coming.

I'd always been like a big sister to Gemma, you see. When she left the home it was me she came to. I had her room all ready. She was happy at first, but being so tiny and all, she always felt inadequate. Then she got a job in a bar. She said the owner was the most honest man she'd ever met. There was nothing false about him; he lived his life according to his rules, and it impressed her. He didn't judge people. Things started to go well for her when she met him.

Then she began staying out a lot, going to clubs and spending the night with a couple of mates in their flat. I'd be at work when she'd get in the following morning. A change of clothes and she'd be away again. We were very close, but, you know, people move on, form new relationships. Gemma could be very secretive about her new friends – insecurity I'd always put it down to, as if introducing them to me would make her less the centre of attraction.

Only that wasn't it this time.

She'd begun spending a lot more money than she was earning and when I asked her about it she told me she'd quit her job and was working for a man called Ted Lyle.

When I said it must be some job, 'It's in the town' was all I could get out of her.

'Where in the town?' was met with 'It's none of your business.'

'Gemma,' I said, 'what's going on? What's wrong with me asking you where you work?'

And then it all came out.

She told me they'd set her up in the hotel and that her old boss was being very good about the whole thing. He had this way of making her feel positive about herself, saying that she should capitalise on her strong points and not feel that she was doing anything wrong.

I'd misread him. I'd thought he would have been against what she was doing. A couple of other girls from a home had got drawn in by the easy money too. Things changed between us after that. I was now seen as the 'disapproving' big sister. I suppose I was. Oh, she didn't think I was a prude or anything like that – if girls want to work hotels, that's up to them – just that I was angry at what she had allowed herself to become when she could have been so much more.

If this had been anywhere but that hotel room she'd have been a bundle of nerves at getting that letter, and I'd have sat beside her while she opened it, willing it to be the news she was hoping for. But I knew she wanted me to leave in case some client turned up and embarrassed her even more in front of me. She was feeling uneasy and wanted me to go and, once the letter was read, she knew I would.

> Dear Gemma,
>   I'm sorry for taking so long to reply to your letter. But as much as I wish things were different, they are what they are, and to welcome you back into my life at this time would not be possible. My family are unaware of my past and, for their sake, I have to decline your request for us to meet. I do hope you understand and do not judge me harshly.
>
> I wish you all the best in life.
> Angela Reading

It was a terrible letter for any mother to have written. Even the style was cold and dispassionate. 'I have to decline your request.' It had all the indifference of a bank manager turning down a loan application. All I could do was kneel down and put my arms around her and tell her how sorry I was. She was beyond devastated.

Gemma suffered from migraines. The rejection brought one on. Her left eye had almost closed over. A lie down in her own bedroom – without the distractions of that place – with the curtains drawn sometimes helped. Light made it worse. But she said she couldn't face going home and wanted to go for a drink. We would go to a nice quiet bar in the country and have a talk. I decided she should come in my car; we could pick hers up the next day. She would have a shower, I'd go and buy some petrol and by the time I got back she'd be ready.

So I went down to the car park, got her coat and handbag out of her car and put them in mine. She didn't like having her handbag in the room. Her clients were strangers.

A laptop was under her coat, on the passenger seat. Gemma had been too upset to remember to tell me she'd bought one. That was why, I thought. I didn't know at that time it wasn't hers. She'd been talking about buying a computer of her own. She was always on mine. This one seemed very expensive. I put it and her other things in my car and drove to the nearest petrol station.

The attendant filled her up, and I went inside and paid. When I came back, sounds were coming from inside the laptop. The kind they make when they're starting up or reprocessing. If Gemma had left it on by mistake, the batteries would run flat. That's how I was seeing it. I didn't know at that time that it was a specially designed surveillance computer. To me it was just a fancy laptop. I lifted the lid to turn it off. Gemma was on screen. It was live, recording her in her room. She was lying on the bed naked. A man was sitting on top of her, humming. It had sound.

At first I thought it was some kind of sick bondage. Her hands were behind her back and he was taping her mouth.

But as I was pulling on to the dual carriageway and speeding back to the hotel to get her out of there – I was furious at seeing someone treating her like that; I'd make her give it up, to hell with how hard a time she gave me over it – he was putting on a pair of surgical gloves and opening out a wallet of instruments next to her head, taking out a protractor and making some kind of design on her chest. And while I rang reception, he picked up a scalpel and began cutting into the lines the protractor had scored.

But the phone just kept ringing. I was out of my mind. She was trying to get him off her, but he must have been three times her weight.

'Top Towers Hotel …'

He had his hand on her throat, pinning her down, while carving with the other. She was powerless to do anything but watch the scalpel carving.

'… Hold the line please.'

'For fuck's sake answer the phone.'

'Top Towers Hotel.'

'Gemma's being killed. She's in room 720.'

He reached for a saw.

'Is this some sort of practical joke?'

'Gemma's being killed in room 720. Help her. Please. He's killing her.'

And started sawing …

'Oh my God! My God! What room did you say, miss? What room—'

'For fuck's sake – 720. Hurry. He's killing her. He's killing Gemma.'

… into her groin, grating into her bone.

I wish you all the best in life. Angela Reading.

I sped back into the hotel car park to run and help her, even though I knew she was beyond help – no one could survive what he had done to her – but when the car came to a halt, he was there, stepping in front of it, out of nowhere, glaring at me through the windscreen then lunging at my door.

All I could do was get away from there as fast as I could, go straight to the nearest Garda station, but he was getting into a Transit van and coming after me, and the traffic going towards the city was thick and wouldn't let me out. If I joined it, I'd be locked in it, and he would catch me. By taking the country road going out of the city, I might be able to outrun him. It was the only route open to me. And it led to Clonkeelin, which no one but me knew about. If I could lose him, I could ring the police from my holiday cottage. Or on the way.

Only I'd made the mistake of thinking that he'd

picked Gemma randomly. I thought he'd seen her working the hotel and gone up to her room. It never occurred to me that he knew her. Knew us both. That he'd been watching us.

If I'd known that, I'd never have gone to Clonkeelin. When I eventually lost sight of his Transit in my rear-view mirror, I thought I'd shaken him off, not that he'd realised I was going to my cottage and had taken a short cut to wait for me there.

When I reached it, my mobile rang and when I answered it a voice said, 'Lucille, how's it going? I've been looking for you. We've something to discuss,' and then the laptop's built-in phone rang and he said, 'I *hear* you've something belonging to me.'

This man had tricked me. He'd rung both phones and heard the one in the laptop ringing through my mobile and knew I had it. Not that I cared about any of that then. But if I'd known that the laptop was to play such a crucial part in what would happen later, I'd never have got out of the car. I'd have kept driving until I could get to the police.

But I did get out. I hung up and went inside to call 999 and as I was closing the hall door, a voice said, 'Ah, Lucille, I had an idea you were driving in this direction.' And then a spray of some kind hit me and I passed out.

RED DOCK

Ted Lyle is what you call a cowardly bastard. He should've kept that surveillance laptop in *his* car. But he was afraid in case the law got wind and nabbed him. So he kept it in Gemma's. They'd figure it was all her doing and blame the scam on her was how he was looking at it. Naïve, but there you go; that's Ted for you – not one of life's great thinkers.

He'd left it under Gemma's coat, recording, while he stayed in the bar.

All very well and good. Until Greg Swags walked in.

Charlie Swags had two sons. Tony, in his mid-thirties, had about eight years on Greg. Tony's one of these guys who'd gained his position in life on the back of what his dad had achieved. Thought it gave him standing. Fancied himself as a bit of a hard case. People were afraid of him only because they knew that if they went up against him, they'd have to deal with Charlie.

Greg was different. He never got involved in Charlie's operations. Didn't know about the camera set-up. To

Greg, Ted Lyle was in the hotel waiting on a working girl in the normal course of business.

They got talking. Small talk mostly, Greg saying he'd just dropped off his fiancée and called in for a beer on the way home, and 'How's things with you?' crap that I won't bore you with. But somewhere in amongst all this, Gemma's name gets mentioned. Greg says he knows her, in a way that suggests they're good friends, and eventually, when he downs his beer, he tells Ted Lyle he hasn't seen Gemma in a while, that he'll go up and see how she's getting on.

You can never plan for things like this. I had no idea Greg was that friendly with Gemma. Certainly not enough to make him take the trouble of going up to see her.

Anyway, that's the way it went. Greg goes upstairs and Ted heads for the Gents. Ted's got a bowel problem. The cunt's forever in the bog. When he comes out, he passes reception and overhears the receptionist taking a call in the office behind the front desk. And by the state she's in, it's obvious that she isn't taking a reservation.

She's saying something like, 'Speak up, miss. Which room number?' Down goes the receiver, and the receptionist's running into the porter's office screaming, 'There's a girl being murdered in 720. There's a girl being murdered in 720.'

Ted jumps into the lift and when he reaches Gemma's room, the door's open and Greg's lying on the floor. He's not what you'd call covered in blood, but there's enough of it on him to suggest he'd come into contact with Gemma, who's lying on the bed in bits. And Ted's thinking he must've had a bad pint, because suddenly it doesn't wanna stay down. Which means he's in the bog again. But he can't stay in it for long. The law'll be on their way, and he does *not* want Charlie Swags asking him questions like, 'Why the fuck didn't you get Greg out of there before they arrived?' Ted knows that when questions like that turn up, he's wishing he'd brought a toilet with him. So it's, 'Greg, get the fuck up,' while having enough of his wits about him to grab the hidden camera. And up Greg gets, drowsy at first, then one look at Gemma and his legs are giving out on him again, Lyle going, 'Don't look at her, don't look at her,' while following his own advice, and that was that.

They were out of there before the law arrived. Down the fire escape and through the car park. Greg gets in his car, Ted in his, then he remembers the surveillance laptop. No problem. Mr No Problem's got it all figured out. There's fuck all to worry about after all. The evidence of who killed Gemma'll be on the laptop. Everything'll be all right.

But the laptop is gone. It's not in Gemma's car. Things aren't all right after all.

And a cop is turning into the car park with his foot to the floor and his siren blaring and banging into Greg's car as he tries to make for the exit. Lyle legs it and Charlie Swags is back on the phone raving like a lunatic. Now to give you some idea of what I'm talking about here: that nut I mentioned earlier who was on the loose in Dublin. Some TV shrink had said: 'It's not so

much that he attracts his victims, he *abstracts* them,'
which led to him being called 'Picasso'. A reporter later
nicknamed him '*Rip*casso' but it never stuck. Everybody's running around with a nickname in this town,
'Chilly' Winters among them. And because Winters
was still being unreasonable, now, for the first time in
twenty years, by the way Charlie was adding it up, it
soon became clear that Winters had an opportunity to
hit him where it hurt. 'You grab my kid, Charlie, I'll
grab yours.' Has a certain logic to it. Winters knew
Greg was no killer. Winters was acting out of revenge.
And that's what was getting Charlie going.

I'd never heard Charlie in such a state. Usually he's
the coolest bastard you'd ever come across under pressure. 'This is bad, Red,' he was going. 'This is bad.
Winters has enough to put Greg away for life.'

'Look, Charlie,' I said, 'you're worrying about nothing. Picasso's victims are bound to carry his hallmark.
When he strikes again, Greg'll be in custody at the time
and Winters'll have to let him go. I'm amazed he's even
holding him. Greg Picasso? The idea's ludicrous.'

To be honest, I wasn't in much form for this. I'd a
glass of cream soda in my hand. My throat was like
wire wool from a wedding do I'd been at. I'd ended up
staggering home and conking out on the sofa. Half an
hour had gone by since this had happened and what
Charlie was telling me was the first I'd heard of it.
OK, Greg had blood on him, but he'd been in a car
crash, it could have been his own. No witnesses had
seen him in Gemma's room. Fair enough, reception

security cameras would later show him in the hotel, going into the lift. But none of it added up past the fact that Winters had found a Swags on the scene and was holding him for no other reason than that. Hardly hard evidence. It was all a bit hazy. An hour or so later Charlie got back to me with: 'Winters even went to Greg's flat and took his dog, Red.'

'His dog? Why?'

'How the fuck should I know? He's hardly likely to tell me.'

I still didn't know what was going on.

But as far as Charlie's first phone call was concerned, to me it was just a frantic father seeing all sorts of possibilities that didn't exist, with me trying to explain why they never would.

'What do you want me to do, Charlie?'

'Find Picasso.'

'Find Picasso? Charlie, what the fuck do I know about catching serial killers?'

'If anybody can catch him, Red, you can. You always do what you put your mind to.'

'I wouldn't hold out too much hope on this one. The law's been after the cunt for the last eight or nine years and look how far they've got. Anyway, you're not even thinking straight, Charlie. It's the laptop you want. Not Picasso.'

'Why do you say that?'

'Because it recorded him killing Gemma. Which means he doesn't know about the camera. If he did, he wouldn't've killed her on it. And to steal it, he'd first have to know about it. Besides, a guy like that hasn't evaded the law by going around drawing attention to himself breaking into cars and setting off their alarms. With the amount of rooms in that place, any number of people could've seen him.'

'Gemma Small's car wasn't broken into, Red.'

This was getting confusing.

'Look, Charlie, a girl took it.'

'How do you know?'

'You said Ted Lyle heard the receptionist taking a call from a "miss" telling her that Gemma was being killed. How could that miss have known what was going on in Gemma's top-floor room unless she'd been watching it on screen? She couldn't have been in the room. She couldn't have been outside looking up. If she had, she'd've run into reception, not phoned. She'll hand it in. Who the fuck's gonna sit on that type of evidence? Besides, the family of one of his victims put up a reward. That'll make her hand it in if nothing else.'

'What if she doesn't?'

I was hoping he wouldn't ask me that. 'You're thinking she might play the scam? Blackmail Gemma's clients?'

'I would in her shoes.'

'Small-time thieves aren't you, Charlie.'

The laptop held at least a couple of dozen of Gemma's clients. Guys with money. Even a small-timer could squeeze each of them for fifty grand a head. There's over a million in itself.

It was a pity we hadn't told Gemma about the scam.

She could have threatened Picasso with the camera and made him back off. But we couldn't have her going around knowing about it in case it got exposed. Not with Charlie's name behind it. After we'd pulled Gemma from the hotel that night, Charlie would have had her done in. Though he didn't know I'd planned on her being found dead with that suicide note in her pocket. As far as a small-time thief was concerned, one might hit Gemma's clients for small-time amounts. But we'd clean the cunts without them even seeing us. One or two usually crack though. Gemma would be hauled in for questioning. Fuck that. That sort of carry-on can get messy. We couldn't tell her – that's all there was to it.

'Ted Lyle's here with me, Red. He said if a girl has it, it might be a Lucille Kells. He can't think of anyone else who'd have keys to Gemma's car. He's positive it wasn't broken into.'

The one name I didn't want to hear. If I'd known Lucille was gonna be brought into it, I'd've held back on the analysing. I certainly wouldn't have mentioned that 'miss' part. Not that I'd've got away with it for any length of time. Charlie knows me. He knows how quickly I come up with likely possibilities, the way I was doing, thick head or no thick head. He'd have worked it out himself eventually. It would've given me a bit of time though to figure a way to keep him from going after her.

'Listen, Charlie, all we're doing here is speculating. Gimme Kells' details,' I said, as though I'd never heard of her. 'I'll check her out and get back to you.'

'Don't let me down, Red. If there was ever a time I need you to come through for me, it's now.'

'I'll do what I can, Charlie, you know me.'

Down goes the phone. The quick way to find out whether Lucille had it was to give her a call. I rang her mobile. She answered. I said something to keep her on the line, rang the built-in phone in my laptop, heard it ringing and knew she had it with her.

If Charlie thought to do what I'd just done, he'd know she had it for sure.

There was one way out of this. If I could get the laptop and send Winters a printout of Picasso killing Gemma, Greg would be released. All I'd have to do is find some way of making Charlie believe that Lucille'd had fuck all to do with it. But first I'd have to get that laptop back before Charlie sent a squad of men over to take her flat apart looking for it.

PICASSO

My second error, as I shall explain, had to do with Gemma Small and Lucille Kells.

Because *December* was to complete my collection, I was not only keen to portray narcissus as perfectly as is humanly possible, I was also very anxious. This, over and above *Duet*, was to be the culmination of years of work, you understand. Nothing, absolutely nothing, but my best endeavours would suffice. In short, for the first time in my life I was embarking on a project in a high state of agitation. Whereas the weaver of tapestry can unpick and start again and, in the same vein, charcoal can be erased, my instruments, once applied, cannot similarly be retracted. One indelicate stroke and the model is rendered unusable and has to be discarded. Superimposition is, given the nature of skin, out of the question. Mistakes cannot be covered up. Gemma Small was therefore to be a trial run.

While both she and Lucille Kells were admirable in their physical attraction, Lucille was by far the more beautiful. Gemma had a delightful, waif-like allure.

Her demeanour was that of a subjugated child. In a previous incarnation, the product of neglect, she would have epitomised the embodiment of both Ignorance and Want. Had she been dark, she would have made an excellent *December*.

Lucille, on the other hand, was not possessed of a boy-like figure. Dressed in black jeans, Danish sandals and a white, sleeved top, with the natural mahogany streaks in her ebony hair curling in around her breasts, Lucille comported herself in a rather impertinent fashion, yet, in more pensive mood, exuded a confidence and grace which no preparatory school could instil.

On one occasion, while I was seated on a park bench, I watched her giggling at some girlish pun. She was affecting a kind of roll-walk, reminiscent of bicycle pedals smoothly rolling round and round, exemplifying some choreography or other to Gemma. She was so full of life. With her hair flowing down over the narcissus, she would portray *December* perfectly. I was determined, at the earliest opportunity, to apprise her of my intentions.

However, having visited Gemma, I had departed in the belief that Lucille Kells would identify me to the police. I thought my career had ended. She would turn me in. Unless I could take appropriate measures. Alas, my Transit was no match for the speed of her Fiesta.

But then it occurred to me that the direction in which she was travelling indicated that she was intent on visiting a location close to the village of Clonkeelin. A hunch, as it were. And one which proved fruitful. For I had already followed her there and knew exactly which short cut to take to arrive before she did. I welcomed her in my usual fashion.

The following morning, having arranged for her to awaken to the same considerations as Lisa Shine and Jackie Hay, I found myself in a mood of some elation. Not only had I acquired *December*, I had also heard, on the radio, that the police had arrested another man in my place, one Greg Swags, as I had connived; though I was surprised to learn that they had mentioned him by name so soon after the event. This Swags was innocent. Clearly the police did not think so. He would go in my stead, as it were, and Lucille would model for me. I should then have to decide on my future career: retirement or enjoying models in the comfort of my rooms and having them regarded as 'missing persons'. Undoubtedly, if the authorities ever caught up with me, the truth would out. Strange the way things transpire, don't you think?

No one was more surprised than me to find myself still at liberty, I must tell you. Swags had *seen* me. He was a vital witness. Ah well, ours is not to reason why, ours is but to do or … no, I don't think so.

Unfortunately, as luck would have it, my sense of elation was short-lived. But only momentarily. A further bulletin reported that perhaps I had been seen. Second-hand news, as only I knew, because I had been present at the scene. They were clearly referring to Lucille. Which brought the question: whom had she informed? And how, since she was with me? I realised that I was becoming concerned over conjecture. The word 'perhaps' brought relief. No doubt you too spotted the uncertain connotation of its usage. 'Perhaps?' I had been seen or I had not. How does one 'perhaps' see one?

A further bulletin furnished enlightenment:

'A woman rang the front desk of the Top Towers Hotel saying Gemma Small was being killed in room 720. The caller had actually named the deceased. She knew her name.'

How, I wondered. What woman caller? And how could she know what was going on in 720? I decided to ask my guest.

LUCILLE

When I regained consciousness, I was in a cell with no windows. A big black rat was in the corner eating a dead one. Behind the cell door was a crate. A length of timber, nails and a small hammer lay next to it. It had already been shored off with another piece. Another, gnawed through and matted with black hair and blood, stood next to it. Rats' hair. There were rats in the crate, trying to gnaw their way out.

He had put a live one in to feed on a dead one, to let me know what would happen if the others ate their way through. I'd be all they'd have to feed on.

'Hello, Lucille.'

It was him. He had been spying on me through a hole in the door. It opened, he said, 'May I?' and stepped into the threshold, filled it: he was enormous. I felt nauseated just looking at him.

'Would you care to see where I work?'

I was too terrified to even move, let alone answer him.

A dog snarled. Then others started barking.

'Follow me. Come on, no need to be concerned.'

No need to be concerned? He had murdered my best friend and now he was talking to me as casually as if we were sitting in a bar over a quiet drink.

The dog – 'Stay there, Shirley,' he said to her – a big, wire-haired mongrel, was squatting at the bottom of a flight of stairs as I went out behind him, into a corridor with four cells, including mine. The last one contained the rest of the dogs. Five. All as big as the one guarding the exit. He opened their door.

'Stay close to me, Lucille. They're only Shirley's pups.'

Oh, God. There were bones inside on the floor. And they were human. Two dogs were chewing on a ribcage, growling at each other, fighting over it.

The mother came in behind us snarling. Then she stood silent, watching the other sniffing and licking my legs.

'They get excited at times like this. In anticipation.'

They made my skin crawl. But it was the look in the mother's eyes that terrified me the most – she was staring at me, drooling. If it's possible to see in a dog's eyes that she is biding her time, then that was what I saw in hers. I was never as glad to get out of a place in all my life.

He led me through an internal door and down some wooden steps into a lower cellar.

'In here.' We went into a room. 'This is where I work.' He took me straight back out again and into another room. 'And this is my gallery.'

Then he questioned me. I realised what he was doing. The rats and the dogs had been enough to make me tell him anything he wanted to know. But he had quickly shown me his studio and gallery to instil as much extra fear as possible. He wanted quick answers.

'Did you alert the Top Towers' receptionist last evening?'

'Yes.'

'How?'

'I saw you. On camera.'

'On *camera*?'

'Yes.'

I told him all that had happened. He flew into a rage then just as quickly came back out of it. The composure of the man was unbelievable.

'And where is this laptop?'

'In my car.'

'Thank you, Lucille. You are very kind. I'm afraid I have to apologise. I cannot now continue this guided tour. Please make yourself at home down here. I shall see you anon.'

He was gone.

So was I. I'd been telling myself: 'Now don't act the meek and mild female, Lucille. Think about how to get yourself out of here. Crying won't get you anywhere. You need your wits.'

But after all that I'd been through, having found my mother, all that I'd hoped for us, I'd never see her again. And what he'd done to Gemma … I couldn't stop myself. I just crumpled on the floor and wept.

RED DOCK

The question was: where was Lucille when I'd rung her? And where was she now? The lights in her flat were out, and she wasn't answering her home phone.

The obvious answer was she'd gone straight to the law with that laptop – that she and her old man, good old Chilly Winters, were seeing each other for the first time in twenty-odd years without knowing who the other was – that he was studying Picasso's latest release, in which Picasso was starring as the bad guy – that by morning, he'd release Greg and everything would be OK. Only Charlie Swags had men watching the cop shops for her. Grab the laptop off her on her way in, pull the scam and then hand it in. But no one had seen her. She hadn't gone near the law as far as any of us could make out. So where the hell was she?

I picked the cylinder lock to her flat and went inside.

An Irish Holiday Cottages brochure was under her bed. Four had been ticked off, all near Clonkeelin. It was nearly midnight. About an hour and a half had passed since Gemma'd been killed. I rang them, saying

I was a relative desperate to contact Lucille. The third one told me what I wanted to know. So I took a drive out.

Lucille had rented a white stone cottage called Roselawn, near the Donavans, in the townland of Coolylacky. Her car was outside. And that's where I found my surveillance laptop.

To be honest with you, I was surprised to find it. If she knew what I was sure she knew, why, as I've said, hadn't she taken it straight to the law? The only thing I could think of was that it had scared her. She couldn't face questioning so soon after seeing Gemma killed on it. Why else would an ordinary working girl hang onto it? Different for someone like me, who could put it to good use.

Odd, really, that she'd left it in the car though. Then again, the chances of anyone else stealing it that particular night were a bit unlikely. Maybe that was how she was seeing it. You have to look at things the way other people do. She might not have wanted it inside with her. All the same, she was surprising me. The lights were out. Seemed a bit unlikely that she'd gone to bed. Out in the country, pitch-black outside, the slightest rustling noise easily heard, it was spooky, especially with images of your best friend being killed still fresh in your mind.

Anyway, she'd no reason to suspect my motives, since she didn't know me. So I couldn't know about Clonkeelin as far as she was concerned. To her, no one knew about it, no one who'd come after her. She'd feel safer there than in town. She'd probably been in such a state that she'd just driven out, closed the bedroom curtains and gone to bed without thinking it through. No reason in the world to suspect I knew all about her.

That's all I could come up with. It didn't make a lot of sense, but very little about this made sense.

It told me of course that she'd already taken steps into her past. There'd been no need for me to arrange for Gemma to be killed. OK, Picasso saw to her, as it turned out. But if I'd known Lucille had gone to Clonkeelin, I wouldn't have set Gemma up in that scam. Picasso wouldn't have found her in the hotel. Don't think this is conscience talking. That's not what I'm about. Fuck it, it happened, that's all.

I took the laptop back to my place for a spot of late-night viewing. Pleasant dreams, Lucille.

Now let's get things in perspective here. Just because you have a laptop that shows Picasso in a hotel room doesn't mean you know who he is. All you have is a face; possibly even a disguised one. It wasn't as if I could plaster it on *Crimefile* asking viewers to call in or go rapping on doors. A face in Dublin, a city of a million faces, was all I had. No name, address, nothing. I could hand it in to Winters, as I've said, but I wanted to look at it first and have a think.

I put my feet up, opened a can of beer and enjoyed the feature.

On the screen, Gemma came out of the bathroom naked. A knock on the door. She pulled on a dressing gown, and because the camera wasn't trained on the door it didn't show her opening it. It had sound though. Sound is handy for blackmailing people. Not only do men not want their wives seeing them fucking around, they don't want them hearing the embarrassing tripe they come out with either.

'Good evening,' a man's voice said. 'Hotel maintenance.' It was Picasso.

Gemma asked him if he could come back later.

'I'm afraid the telephone system is dysfunctional. The fault has been traced to your room. Our other guests are being inconvenienced. May I? Shan't take a moment.'

She let him in. The tool bag in his hand made him look like a tradesman. She didn't ask for ID. For all the good it would've done her.

Big guy, he was – any taller and he'd've needed to duck under the light fitting – blonde hair. Hands like baseball gloves. I'd expected him to shut her up with them. But he had other ideas. He put the tool bag on the bed and opened it. Gemma had no sooner turned to go into the bathroom than he drew a spray out of the bag and coughed politely before saying, 'Oh, just one thing more.'

She turned back saying, 'Yes?' and caught it straight in the face.

To say the spray knocked her out would not be entirely accurate. It was trying to knock her out though. She was way beyond swooning and heading towards collapsing when he caught her and laid her out on the bed. Next came a look at what lay beneath her dressing gown. He took it off. I thought for a moment he wouldn't pass up the opportunity to sample what he was admiring, but he had other ways of treating women – sitting on top of her, taping her mouth and binding her hands behind her back. Even if she'd been fit enough to put up a struggle by this time, it would've been useless. He must've had ten stone on her. A weightlifter would've had a job shifting him.

I now got some idea why they'd named him Picasso. Maybe he was a nut who thought he *was* Picasso. That or he thought he was a geometry teacher. He used a protractor on her chest. Then a scalpel. This was why he'd taped her mouth. The spray would've kept her unconscious and therefore quiet. The scalpel brought her round. She was now wide awake and fit to scream the house down and disturb the other guests. He had it all worked out. Oh, there was a lot of holding her face down and generally preventing her from kicking and bucking, but there was still a fair bit of composure in what he was enjoying. He reminded me of a barber with a careful hand on the cut-throat razor. Only he wasn't shaving her, he was ... sketching. There's no other word for it. It might sound mad, but what I was reminded of was that artists not only paint, they sketch. And Picasso sketched with scalpels. No way could this guy be copycatted; not by any professional killer I knew. The artistic element ruled it out. You'd need to see the flair with which he'd used those blades to know what I mean.

Next came a saw. He kept his tools surgically clean.

This one was pristine. A tenon saw, the kind you'd use for sawing mitre joints. He had other joints in mind. Her groin to start with. She wasn't objecting now. She was way past objecting.

I stilled the frame and – now this bit was part speculation; my surveillance gear was good, but it wasn't good enough to show minute detail – because I was watching this on a computer screen and not on a VCR, I was able to enhance a shot of a cellophane bag he'd taken out of the tool bag along with his camera. I couldn't tell for sure, but to me it looked like the bag contained a tongue. In clear liquid. A big tongue. I thought of a dog's, only because I'd expected to see a 'dog' element in this. Winters had taken Greg's. He hadn't taken it for a walk. It had to have some connection. Fuck knows what it was.

But it occurred to me that if I were a killer like him, what would I do with a tongue? More importantly, what would *he* do with it? Working out in the open, he might bring a dog along to lick the victim. He'd be too smart to draw attention to himself by walking into the Top Towers Hotel with one on a lead. Would he bring a tongue instead? Would licking a victim with it be his way of avoiding copycats? If the liquid was saliva, would it come from one mutt in particular? Without that ingredient, no one could copy his work. Flair or no flair. Forensic'd spot it. That's how I saw this anyway.

By this time, y'see, I'd been toying with the idea that if I couldn't catch him, I could copycat him. If a girl turned up carrying his hallmark, Greg'd be released and the pressure'd be off. And if I did manage to track him down later on – I'd come up with one idea – he'd be available to do a bit of work for me now and again. No point wasting a perfectly good scalpeler. Angles. Always see the angles. But copycatting was now definitely a non-runner. Even if I had his expertise, no way could I get hold of that particular saliva, if that's what it was.

Getting back to what he was doing to Gemma, Greg Swags interrupted him, knocking on the door maybe. The sound of knocking didn't come through because of the noise the saw was making. What happened exactly I couldn't see. Picasso went off camera. My guess is he looked through the peephole, saw Greg, opened the door and caught him unawares. Dig in the gut, something like that. Then dragged him in. I saw that bit. Greg was doubled up, not out. That came when Picasso hit him across the back of the head with the coffee table. Then he put away his tools. Nothing like a neat tradesman. All except for a scalpel – he put that between Greg's fingers then slung it behind the settee. So that's why Chilly Winters was still holding Greg. His prints on the scalpel. Strengthened his case nicely. Picasso had set Greg up. That was it. Then he pulled off his bloodstained sweater and surgical gloves and was out the door.

This bastard was impressing me.

I got a few hours' kip then went to see Charlie Swags. I wasn't sure whether or not to tell him I'd found the laptop. If I did, I'd have to tell him I'd taken it off

Lucille. Which meant I'd have to say where she was. She'd be dead if I did that.

Now things with me and Charlie weren't the same as they used to be. Years ago, before he got to be as big as he was now, we used to work closely together. I'd do most of the thinking, and he'd supply the muscle. We'd get into a few scrapes, but y'know how it is – it comes with the job. The laughs had gone. These days he'd come to me for a favour, like that thing with Drake, I'd think up a plan, then he'd tell his hired help to carry it out. I'd get a cut, but that would be it. Whether or not he'd see it like that, I don't know. It was how I saw it though. He was above himself.

I'll give you an idea of what I mean. Take security. Charlie's security mad. You have to press the intercom button at the entrance gate and say the magic words 'Red Dock' before his honchos'll let you in the fucking place. Big house with pointy roofs on all sides, big lawns, high perimeter walls. The Irish president has fewer heavies. Charlie even has bulletproof windows in his Merc. And a black Merc too. Maybe the cunt thinks he *is* the president. You'd understand it if he was forever ducking, but nobody's taken a shot at him in years.

Not my type of house though. Didn't fancy it. Some big-shot bishop used to live in it. All arched windows and grey scabbled stone. Lose your key and you'd need a battering ram to open the fucking door. Imagine living in a house a bishop used to live in, for fuck's sake. I dunno, some people get grand ideas.

112

'Red?'

'Kane, how's it going?'

Jerry Kane. Charlie's head man. Give him the wrong answer to 'Who the fuck're you?' and your dentist bills go up. A guy hit him with the head one night and knocked himself out. Just as well – Kane would've buried him. He'd called Kane 'Chinky eyes'. Kane's what you might call Charlie's chief clearer-upper. If Charlie says 'Kane'll take care of it', it usually means some insurance company's about to pay out on a life policy.

I was wearing my 'Fuck me, things are bad' face, in light of the day's events, Greg arrested and all. So was Kane, though he always looks like that.

'Charlie's waiting for you, Red. He's out the back.'

'Right.'

As I crossed the hall, Charlie's wife was in what she calls the 'drawing' room, tinkling the grand piano, which none of them could play, with one hand, a glass of something in the other. I put my head in the doorway and nodded hello. She looked up and waited, as much as to say, 'Any news that'd help Greg?' I shrugged, meaning no. Back she went to Three Blind Mice. They sounded drunk as well. My guess was she was also on Valium.

Oddly enough, it was she who'd introduced me to Charlie. Years ago when I was in my teens, I fancied myself as a private detective. She'd hired me to see if he was up to anything. So I tailed him and then purposely let him see me. He grabbed me by the throat and said, 'What the fuck's the crack?' and I said, 'Well, Charlie, we're all trying to make a few shillings.' I indicated that his good lady was concerned about their marriage vows in relation to him fucking other women then let him talk me into keeping my mouth shut. For a consideration. I told his wife he was a saint, billed her as well and got paid twice. I had to or she'd've wondered why not. A small scam. But there's always an angle if you go looking for it.

Sabina her name is – though everybody calls her 'Bin'. A decent-looking redhead in her prime. But after years of sixty a day and a couple of goes at the facelifting, with the odd tuck here and there, the word 'prime' gets relegated. The old story – big shot keeps wife around because she's the mother of his kids. Any lip and she knows the result. So she keeps her tongue in her head and her position – the wife of Charlie Swags. She'd settled for it.

The 'back' was like the Botanic Gardens' greenhouse: the love of Bin's life now that Charlie no longer gave two fucks whether she hired private investigators to follow him. You can always tell when a marriage's fucked: the humour dies. Once a man stops pulling his wife's leg, it's usually because he's pulling somebody else's. Ever notice that? A guy goes with a girl, proposes, marries and everything's great, light-hearted. He's got a funny side to him. Then stodge creeps in and it's all very mundane; the only jokes she hears come from the TV. From then on in, it's sharing everything but sparkle. Fuck that.

Charlie wasn't much of an improvement. Everything he came out with had a big sigh on the end of it. 'Red,

114

how's it going?' sounded like 'Fuck me, poor Greg, what're we gonna do?' Depressing. It would've taken more than a beauty clinic to lift his face. And he'd been up all night by the look of him. Usually by this time – it was getting on for nine – he'd be turned out like a tailor's dummy, darting the cuffs and setting the tie. No tie today. A string vest and suit trousers. I could've done with taking my shirt off as well. Now I know why Bin hadn't an ounce on her. It was fucking roasting in there. Tarzan would've felt at home.

Charlie pulled me up a wicker chair and nodded to the booze on the glass-topped coffee table. 'Help yourself, Red.'

'No thanks, Charlie.' I didn't fancy any. As usual, he was on Irish Mist. He downed what was in his glass and poured himself another, then out came the smokes. I don't touch them. Charlie's one after the other. He was always the same. They were telling on him too. His chest always sounded like a mouthful of phlegm was on the way.

I asked him where Ted Lyle was.

'Fuck Ted Lyle. Letting Greg walk in on the like of that. If Winters doesn't finish the bastard, I will.'

Which meant Winters had since hauled him in.

'What does your brief say, Charlie?' Charlie had the best legal firm in Dublin watching out for him. They'd be working on getting Greg bail.

'Winters is putting severe pressure on that son of mine, Red.'

'Oh?'

The implication was obvious, though not one that I was gonna dress a question around. Not that I couldn't have. I was one of the few people who could get away with asking Charlie a direct personal question without him taking it as a slight. A fool might've asked him if he meant that Greg might squeal on Charlie's activities in return for a deal. Charlie would've taken it like a dig in the mouth, the fool seen as showing no respect and advised to leave. A look would've done it. Charlie's into all that respect stuff. Me, I know what I am: I neither expect nor deserve respect. Charlie thinks he's entitled because he's got a chandelier some aristocrat put up before the bishop moved in. It's all bullshit.

'It's yer woman I'm thinking of, Red.'

'Who?'

'Bin. It's hard for a mother to see her son taken away from her.'

'Sure now …'

'Let alone labelled a killer.'

'Desperate.'

'She has visions of being separated from Greg for the next twenty years. What mother can stand that? And him an innocent party.' Big drag, lips pursed, purple from years of big drags. Charlie was looking old. And creased. Another few years and he'd be seeing a gob like a bloodhound's in the mirror. But you can see what I'm getting at. He was only using Bin to let me know he wanted action. Which wasn't like him. That was probably his second bottle he was digging into and, with no sleep, the old brainwaves were going out on the wrong frequency. Letting me know he wanted this cleared up didn't even need to be said. You could've made condensed soup with it it was that thick.

'You know I have every confidence in you, Red. But maybe you going after Picasso is too much for just one man.' He was telling me that if I didn't come up with a result soon, he'd put others on it. If I knew him, he already had. 'No harm in putting a man in Kells's place to watch for her though.'

'As long as he doesn't fuck things up, Charlie. You know how I work.' Alone.

'I know that, Red. Nobody keeps things to himself the way you do. Or sees things the way you do.'

'Still, it *is* your son we're talking about here. If you want me to step aside, I'll give you what I have, and you can have a think.' I didn't say, 'I'll give you what I have, and you can give it to someone else to run with.' That would've been too firm a recognition on my part that he'd no confidence in me. He also knew that I knew that if he put his heavies, plus an investigator, on to it, they were unlikely to be any more successful than I'd be. He'd then be in the position, further down the line, of having to come back to me to pick up where I'd left off.

With Charlie, things were often expressed through facial gestures and silences. Little is said but a lot implied. He knew he'd handed me a case even the Garda Síochána couldn't solve. And I had to let him think that I was still his best option. Then there was the guilt factor. The sex scam with Gemma was my idea. If

I hadn't come up with it, Greg wouldn't be in this mess. Charlie knew I'd be sensitive to that and do my best.

'You think Lucille Kells has that laptop, Red?'

'She's in the running, Charlie.' I had to say that.

'Find her, Red. If she has it, take the scam off it and use the rest to get Greg out. Then Kane'll take care of it.' There it was. For 'it' read 'Kells'. Bye bye, Lucille. Now you know why I wasn't giving him the laptop.

Bin came in, glass in hand. Serious times. Bin never interrupts, son or no son. Interrupting meant she was telling Charlie she didn't trust his judgement, hadn't confidence in him to get Greg off.

He looked at her as if to say: 'It's only the morning after, Bin, for fuck's sake. Things take time.' On form, I'd expected him to tell her to get lost. Charlie's family's complicated. Families aren't my strong point. You're into deep feelings. I didn't say anything. She knew I'd be seeing this as a first for her and what it implied. Charlie stared at his drink, as much as to say fuck it, I'm going to let this pass; she has a right this time. All to keep the pressure on me to clear up the mess he'd brought about through Drake. Not that he'd be looking at it like that. Charlie's a great one for creating an atmosphere where the blame gets shifted from him onto someone else.

Bin looked ready for crying, yet determined to fight it back. I wanted out of there. Yappy women get on my tits. Here she was: 'What does this Lucille Kells look like? Do you even know that, Red?' *Do you even know that?* See what I mean? What had been said before I'd arrived, I couldn't say, but he'd let her think I was more to blame than he was. Not that she was shouting or anything. This was more a case of a mother not being told *all* the facts and knowing she wouldn't be. She'd been eavesdropping, had heard the name 'Lucille Kells' and grabbed it. She might even have heard the words 'scam' or 'laptop'. Whatever they were linked to, all she wanted was her son back and knew she'd largely be kept in the dark about the circumstances that lay behind it.

'So what *have* you got, Red?' Bin asked. Jesus I hate that tone. 'I asked you if you even know what she looks like?' 'Even', like 'have', had sarcasm wrapped around it.

'Only by the photographs in her flat, Bin.'

Which told her I'd been there and seen them. Where she intended going with this I hadn't a clue. She hadn't enough info to take it far. I decided to use it to keep her quiet.

I hit her with what Charlie had indicated. 'This only happened last night, Bin. It'll take time to figure out.'

'Greg will be delighted to hear that.'

Yeah, well, that's the way it goes, Bin. No point having a go at me. I have my own problems. If Charlie ever gets wind I'm sitting on the laptop, Kane'll be 'taking care of it' boot-firsting me over some fucking cliff.

It just goes to show what families are really like. For a lot of years I'd kept Charlie out of jail by planning jobs that he otherwise would've fucked up and got done for. Charlie's streetwise and the best at what he does

119

– inspiring terror in others; the cunt's a terrorist – but he's no *Mastermind* contestant. Where did she think this fancy gaff came from? The grand in the 'drawing room'? The nightclubs and the whole pile? I helped build it. And what do I get for it in return? Sarcasm.

I'd always be an outsider to her. Welcome me during good times, occasionally, have a dig at me during bad. There's no percentage in it. This time I was putting myself first. I'd get Greg off when the time came. I had the evidence at home. But only after I'd dealt with *my* family – for a change. If this doesn't tell you how our 'relationship' – I hate the intimacy of that word – had weakened over the years, I don't know what will. Sure I was still the guy who was closest to Charlie. Sure I was still high up in his 'organised crime', as Winters liked to label it, with his: 'Charlie Swags *is* organised crime in this city'. And that wouldn't change. But I was still an outsider. A couple of weeks in custody wouldn't do Greg any harm as far as I could see.

LUCILLE

His studio contained everything you'd expect: easel, palette, brushes, canvas. A zinc-topped table sat in the corner, draped in bloodstained velvet. Beside it an upright fridge-freezer. It contained human hands in plastic bags. Eleven in a row. All right. Three fingers had been cut off each one; only the indexes and thumbs remained, each labelled with their victim's name and that of a flower.

On a lower shelf lay two more hands, labelled Jackie Hay and Lisa Shine. Their fingers had not been removed.

A tongue in a cellophane bag lay on the bottom shelf: a dog's.

His wallet was in a chest of drawers. It contained scalpels of various sizes and the protractor he'd used on Gemma. The surgical saw was in the next drawer along with an album full of photographs of his victims, taken after he'd finished with them. A camera sat next to them.

A second album, of newspaper clippings and magazine articles, confirmed that he was Picasso.

All the paintings in the gallery were of girls. One had had her arms and legs removed and rearranged like spiders' legs around her upright torso. Another had Medusa's head, only with fingers instead of snakes. All the girls' heads were slightly bowed to the side. Several wore nuns' veils. Others wore Christian Brothers' belts, complete with crucifixes tucked into them. Every girl had a flower on her chest. One a rose, the next one a carnation and so on. Eleven singles, plus one double – a portrait of two girls. It hung in the centre of the main wall: *Duet*.

None was signed. Each had been stamped with a handprint, before the oil had dried. Of the singles, Gemma would have made twelve. He had been carving a flower into her chest.

Below *Duet* stood a leather-bound lectern. On it sat a journal. It contained the names of the girls, addresses and personal details, the nights they'd been abducted, how they'd been abducted. Girls who had been killed but not painted had the words 'unsatisfactory models' written beside their names.

He had portrayed them all as ugly, grotesque and distorted. All except Medusa. She had two faces, one of a beautiful nun, the other – on the back of her head – of Medusa herself, reflected in a mirror in the background, in which was yet another reflection, of Jesus holding the hand of a frightened boy with blond hair, much like Picasso's own. The boy had gone to Jesus for protection, but the nun's Medusa face was turning Jesus into a statue of stone.

The different flowers on the girls' chests represented the months of the year, according to the journal. The girls in *Duet*, portrayed limbless, who sat facing each other kissing, arms and legs plaited and briered to form a girdle of thorns around their waists, were friends of Gemma's. Jackie Hay and Lisa Shine. They'd disappeared while walking their Labrador.

You may guess how the paintings affected me. Viewing them in a public gallery would be one thing, but when you're condemned to be in one of them, well ... I had seen how he had used his scalpels on Gemma while she was still alive, how he would use them on me. I had seen how I would be represented in death.

I'd come to understand my role in this. My hand would lie next to the others. It would be labelled and that label would carry my name and the name of a flower he would carve in my chest.

I was to be *December*.

'Hello, Lucille.'

Picasso was back.

RED DOCK

The time had come to deal with the Donavans, and to do that I needed to find Lucille. I no longer saw any point in trying to understand why she hadn't gone straight to the law when Gemma was killed. To me, she hadn't gone, she'd stayed in her cottage, and that was that. I will say this: kids ran away from orphanages in Ireland for decades. They went to the law for help, weren't believed and the law brought them back. Lucille would know that. If she saw the laptop had gone from her car and didn't trust the law, why go to them if the evidence had been nicked? From her viewpoint, she'd get her name and picture in the paper; she'd have to explain Clonkeelin. Picasso would see it. Would Lucille want that bastard trying to track her down? Leading him to those she thought were her family? Complicated. Who knows what's in a young girl's mind?

I was parked in a lane a quarter of a mile away looking down at her cottage through a pair of binoculars. There was no sign of her. But her car was in the drive and the bedroom curtains were still closed. She had to be in there. An hour later there was still no sign. There was an agricultural show on in the village. Maybe she'd gone to it, walked in. In her state of mind, I couldn't see her going to it, but it wouldn't take long to have a look.

Not the first show I'd ever been to. I won't describe it. I'm sure you know what a field with a load of spruced-up farm animals looks like. Brother Conor was there, talking to a guy with a bull, a dopey rosette in its ear. Anne was showing a mare in what the programme I had to buy to get in said was the 'mare in foal' class. 'Clonkeelin Lady' she had it listed under. A big grey Irish Draught with a white blaze down its face. Lucille wasn't to be seen.

I tried the bar – a beer tent with a counter on barrels.

My mouth was still dry from that wedding. A pint would cure it. I stood beside my two sisters at the bar. Not as much as a glance did they give me. Not even a 'Here, don't you look like one of us? The resemblance is amazing.' I could've been a statue in O'Connell Street for all they knew. Anne came in and went over to them.

'Now sure you know yourself, Amy,' the man with them was saying. He was their age, late fifties with a well-trimmed tache.

I'd seen him with them many a time – he and Amy in particular were into going to dances – usually down the local after all the twos, all the sixes and eyes down for a full house. I'd spent long enough planning this to know all about them.

'I do well, Cormac,' said Amy, her auburn hair lacquered up like a crash helmet. 'And what do you think,

125

Edna? Cormac and meself always have a good time, don't we, Cormac? Eh, and what do you think, Edna?'

'Sure now,' said big Edna. I doubt she was even listening. The Guinness to her lips and the cigarette lining up to take its place had her attention. She downed what was left of it and cocked her cabbage haircut at the barman, showed him her glass then waved a finger in the direction of the others for another round.

'So we're on, then?' said the tache, palming his hair. A guitar has more strands to it.

'I'd say we are,' said Amy, and her with the blush. The hairdo was obviously for Cormac, her dance-hall Romeo. 'Edna?'

Edna seemed to have the shout on this outing. But she was still thinking it over, a bob of the cabbage, a, 'Hm, maybe', a drag on her non-tipped.

'Sure we'll have a grand time, the three of us,' said the guitar string.

'Edna?' Amy asked.

Edna replied with a big shrug, then, 'G'on. Might as well. Nah. Maybe not. You two go on yourselves.' *Very* decisive.

'That settles it so,' said Amy's fancy man, 'Saturday night it is,' and had a drink. Amy smiled like a young girl who'd just been asked to her first dance, while Edna wondered 'Where t'fuck's that barman?'

Another waste of time. I already knew what my darling family did for kicks. Some guy squeezed in-between them and started asking Anne about her mare. A prospective buyer trying to find out if she was thinking of selling the foal out of Clonkeelin Lady. I'm sure you already know horsey people do that all the time. If the sire and dam are prizewinners, the chances are they'll produce one for the ring. Anne told him her mare had six weeks to go.

Still no sign of Lucille.

I went back to my perch and watched her place for a while, gave it a couple of hours then tried the cottage phone. No answer. Fuck it. I went in.

A metal spatula to unlock the latch on the transom of the sash window and I was standing in her living room. Nothing. She wasn't in any of the other rooms either. The bed hadn't been slept in.

A mobile rang on my way back out, through the hall. A small vase had been knocked off its table. Flowers had fallen out of it, and the carpet was wet. An accident? Lucille had opened the door and bumped into it? Who knows? The mobile lay next to it. I checked the incoming number on the display, let it ring out then rang the number back.

Chilly Winters answered. 'Winters.'

Winters had rung her.

Me and him aren't talking, so I hung up. I was glad I hadn't answered it – he knew my voice. And he'd obviously done his homework and knew about Lucille. He was bound to anyway. If I could work out that she'd made the call to the Top Towers, so could he.

The mobile rang again. I pressed the button this time, but didn't say a thing. 'Lucille? Lucille, I know you've just rung me. This is Detective Sergeant Winters.

Lucille, it's vital you contact us about last night. Your life may be in danger. Lucille?'

If that didn't tell me she hadn't been to see him, nothing would.

I checked her car. Gemma's handbag was under a coat on the back seat. In the boot was a suitcase containing Lucille's clothes. Milk, coffee, cereal and things were in a box. Who the hell moves into a holiday home and leaves their gear and stuff outside?

I went back to my car and waited.

Know the problem with weighing up every possibility in sight but ignoring the unlikely ones? The unlikely ones don't add up. They only add up when some unknown factor arrives and you say to yourself: ah, so that's what happened; that explains it. Well, an unknown factor was arriving. How he'd found out about Clonkeelin, I couldn't even begin to guess since only me and Lucille knew about it. But there he was. Unless, like me, he had a twin, Picasso was getting out of a Transit and going into Lucille's driveway.

OK, I could speculate as to what I *now* thought was going on here, but I'd be wasting your time. I didn't know. What I did know was that Picasso went straight for Lucille's car and he was searching it in a way that told me that whatever it was he thought he was after, that's where it was. Every inch of it. And the only way he could've known that the laptop – he had to be after that – was in it was by being told. And the only one who knew it was in there was Lucille.

He'd grabbed her.

128

The question was: would he lead me to her? Or to put it another way: was there anything left of her that was worth being led to?

I'd already been back through the laptop of course. Twenty-six different clients were recorded on it. I'd figured maybe Picasso had been one of them. Most of their names and addresses were listed. Ted Lyle had checked out some of their financial details and had listed them on the hard disk, together with personal stuff, wives' names, kids and grandkids, in some cases. I'd thought Picasso might have first got to know Gemma by picking her up at an earlier date and going up to her room as just an ordinary punter. By the way he'd gone straight to her room the night he killed her, he had to have known exactly where to find her. How did he know that? Anyway, like everything else, it hadn't given me the answers I'd been looking for. So I tailed him.

To be honest, even if he hadn't grabbed Lucille, he was bound to try. The news on the radio'd said that a young woman had rung reception and had called Gemma by name. Lucille was her flatmate. He'd have worked it out that she might have been the caller and gone after her. So I'd expected to catch up with him one way or the other, even if it meant waiting until Gemma's body'd been released for burial. He'd think Lucille would go to the funeral. He'd snatch her there. Bound to. She was the only one who could ID him, if I was reading this right.

I'll tell you something else about him – when I saw him first on that laptop, a feeling of déjà vu hit me. I was sure I knew the bastard from somewhere. An older version of someone I'd met years ago. Couldn't place him though.

Oddly enough, when that funeral did eventually take place – a small cortège it was, Gemma not having any family, just a bunch of mates and a couple of newspaper and TV people – I saw one woman there who got into a car with a Longford plate. Angela Reading maybe. Winters might've found that letter of mine and phoned Angela to tell her that the daughter she'd written to was being buried. Wonder what her response was. Denied all knowledge of course. Crying her eyes out she was. Everybody's got a story to tell.

For now I stuck with Picasso's.

I followed him to a detached house in an avenue out the Cork road – what you might call leafy middle-class suburbia. And a bit with it if some of the cars were anything to go by. No car in Picasso's driveway though. And that Transit of his looked out of place in this setting. Whoever owned that house could afford better than his set of wheels. I doubt he lived there. And I needed to know exactly where he did live before paying it a visit.

A taxi arrived at around seven and picked up Picasso and an elderly woman. I followed them to the Shelbourne hotel, parked just outside in St Stephen's Green and watched them go inside to the restaurant, to a nice table for two by the window. I went in by the side entrance, had a Powers whiskey in the Horseshoe Bar before choosing a quiet table in the corner, not far from theirs, and ordering a steak and a pint of beer. Hungry work this tailing business.

He looked heavier this close up, wore a pilot's jacket with the zip down, cords and sneakers. His hair, blond of course, was bushy and needed a cut, and he had a baby's face, chubby, as were his hands, small podgy nose and deep-set eyes. If he'd had a romper suit on, he'd have looked like a big toddler. And there was something in those eyes: dark, menacing and sinister. No there wasn't. I'm only joking. He didn't look any more menacing than the waiter who brought my sirloin: rare, just the way I like it. Blood on the knife, just the way Picasso likes it.

I couldn't hear much of their conversation. He seemed to have other things on his mind – not getting caught, for one. She did most of the talking, rather like a mother advising her son to make something of his life was how it came across, for all he ever did was nod 'Yes, Mother, no Mother.' All very formal: a well-dressed old girl deferred to by her boy.

I kept wondering about how he'd targeted his women. He'd certainly targeted Gemma. Maybe he learnt their habits, where they worked, formed a pattern then rapped their doors. Knew exactly where to go. Whatever way he did it, he'd managed to outwit the likes of Chilly Winters for long enough. Smart. I like that. A bit of thinking impresses me, as opposed to some caped nut straight out of nineteenth-century Whitechapel, who strikes from the shadows then flees at the first sign of a screaming passer-by. Mind you,

Jack the Ripper never got caught either, as all those films about him keep reminding us.

I paid my bill, saw his mother paying theirs and made a point of leaving first. A taxi took them back to the leafy avenue, where Picasso went inside for a minute or two then drove off.

He didn't live in Dublin. I followed him to a farm-house at the end of a long lane a couple of miles outside a village called Shantallagh. And there he stayed. I had a bed to go to myself. I was knackered. It had been a long day.

OK, you're wondering why I didn't go in and save Lucille, or call in Swagsy & Co to do as much themselves. That's the good guy's job. I'm the bad guy. You have to hate me in all this. I'm the guy you have to detest. You read about people like me in True Crime stories, not in please-love-my-character fiction. Remember that. It might give you some idea of what makes me the way I am.

Besides, if he'd already scalpeled her, there was nothing I could do about it. And if he hadn't, he wouldn't. Not until he got that laptop back. She was his only source of information as far as that was concerned. Once that changed, then he'd see to her.

Nah. He was smart. On form, she'd be dead. While she was of another use to him, he'd leave his scalpels in the drawer.

If you knew the one overriding reason I had for doing this, you might understand. But since I don't give a fuck whether you understand or not, my reasons are my own.

But let me run this one by you. If you have a brother, look at him now. What would you do for him? Or, putting it another way, what would you *not* do for him?

Now place yourself, think yourself, if you can, into the basest level of humanity where all that exists is misery and deprivation. Then go lower. Seek out those depths. There you might find where I come from.

Now look again at your brother. Imagine him gone. Imagine him still down there. He's nine years old and he's terrified. Would you want to bring him back up, away from it all? Away to a place that is sweet and natural? A place where he wants to be? Yes? Then you love him as much as I loved Sean. We're no different. I just have the mentality of those depths, that's all. There was a time when I didn't. And I didn't instil that mentality in myself.

LUCILLE

'Lucille?'

When Picasso came back, the fear of him made me pass out. He'd carried me back to my cell.

'Yes?'

'In your pocket I found a birth certificate accompanied by a note from a Sister Joseph.'

'Lucille Kells is not my real name.'

'You are connected to the Donavan riding stables?'

'Yes.'

'Your mother is Anne Donavan?'

'That's what it says.'

'Then why were you living in a holiday home and not—'

'They don't know who I am. I didn't tell them. I didn't tell anyone about Clonkeelin.'

'Kells carries with it a religious connotation, as in *The Book of Kells*.'

'So?'

'I myself have had some experience similar to that of your own. An old acquaintance of mine had formed the theory that abandoned children, those without known backgrounds, as opposed to you, with one, were named by the religious *of* the religious?'

'I only know they named me Kells.'

'Hmm, interesting, though perhaps not relevant.'

I didn't understand what he was getting at.

'Now: the laptop computer. Yours?'

'No.'

'Then whose?'

'What will you give me?'

He laughed. 'You are indeed a product of your upbringing. You have played this game before.'

'Not voluntarily.'

'Quite. Voluntarily connotes choice, a right denied you.'

'Where did *you* learn it?'

'Excellent: engage with your persecutor, humour him and it might go easier on you. Respond only, and remain solely in the position of the subjected. You are very clever. The same environment as yourself.'

He'd said he'd had a similar upbringing.

'You've taken it to extremes.'

'The goal is the same, Lucille: pressure applied to extract that which is not volunteered. Psychological persuasion, one might say. A technique which I have also studied. In your case for sexual favours?'

'Given against my will.'

'Of course. Which some blatantly demanded, while others used cunning – those of the "don't tell" fraternity. Puzzling. Since no one would believe you, and since they saw to it that you never *could* tell, the dictum was thus rendered academic.'

'And in yours?'

He didn't answer. Since he'd brought it up, I took it that he'd undergone 'psychological persuasion'. Mental torture, I would call it. We'd both been abused as children, a topic I'd rather not go into. You do your best to live through it, that's all. I do not blame the Church. God did not abuse me – those who abused the position He had given them did.

'Your instinct for survival has not deserted you, Lucille.'

'Sometimes instinct is all you have to go on.'

'And yours is telling you to …?'

'I'll answer your questions for another length of timber.' The rats were scaring the life out of me. 'In case you should go out and be delayed.'

'I shall try not to be. Go on.'

'I think the laptop belongs to a man called Ted Lyle. Gemma worked for him.'

'Her pimp?'

'Yes.'

'He was blackmailing her clients?'

'I don't know that for sure.'

'Yet if, as you say, you told no one of Clonkeelin, then how did Lyle know where to go to retrieve his computer? It's gone from your car.'

'I didn't tell him. I don't even know Ted Lyle – only by sight.'

'Nor I. Yet. I shall pay him a call.' The door opened. 'Your payment.'

136

'Thank you.'

'Anon.'

I now had two pieces of timber.

I waited for an hour or so until I was sure I couldn't hear him walking around on the floor above me then took the only chance I could see of getting out of there.

The walls of the cell were modern concrete block, but on the other side of the door the masonry was much older. No daylight came from any direction into the corridor. I had to be in a cellar. The house had to have two. If the ceiling above me was plaster, joist and floorboards, maybe I could just find a way out.

I put the claw of the hammer onto the edge of the first piece of replacement timber and hit it with the second one until it split then broke the split length into pieces. Using three of the four nails, I nailed them to the second one and made treads to make a kind of ladder.

The crate was to the left of the door, which meant that when Picasso opened the door, the crate was behind it. I took the risk that he wouldn't see that piece of ceiling to the side almost above his head. If he looked up, my plan wouldn't work.

I put my home-made ladder at an angle on the top of the crate, climbed up to the ceiling and began scoring a square in its plaster. It would take time.

The problem was the rats. If they ate their way through, I'd have only one nail to shore off the crate. It wouldn't be enough.

RED DOCK

The following morning I was back watching Picasso's place, though it was well into the evening by the time he drove away in his Transit. Time to go up and have a look.

His front door had a lock on it like something you'd see in a dungeon. I couldn't pick it. Cylinders and modern mortises are about my limit. His back one had a cylinder. And it wasn't his only line of defence. A monster was roaming the downstairs, a cross between a big dog and an even bigger big dog. Huge slobbery mouth on it too. Didn't fancy it. It had jaws that'd bite clean through your wrist.

Now as you well know, the best way to deal with a dog is to put your boot up its arse. But not when its arse is as high off the ground as your own. I've used a device the makers call 'Scare Away', though I don't carry it with me. It's about the size of a car battery and gives out a sonic pitch only dogs can hear. Makes them act like they're hearing terrible news and back off. It works only on nine out of ten dogs though. This one might've been the tenth.

I used it on an old woman once. She lived next door to a bank job I was setting up. We needed her kitchen wall for the purposes of gaining entry. And, in keeping with my no-fuss methods, she had to be out of the house. Fortunately her husband had just dropped dead and she was all alone with their faithful Kerry Blue Terrier. So I installed the 'Scare Away' treatment in their bedroom. The dog wouldn't enter it. She thought it was her hubby's spirit. Dogs being able to see spirits that we can't. Because only the dog could hear it, it kept her awake night and day howling. She had to go and stay with her daughter for rest and recuperation. And came back and found a big hole in her wall. Of course, you're probably saying to yourself: why didn't he just hit her over the head with something? I would have, but I wanted to try out my experiment.

Another way to fend off dogs of course is to use a warden's loop or maybe a dart gun or a shield – one that looks like a big upside-down cheese grater. They lunge at you and cut their paws to bits on it. Handy if you like grated paws. The best method I've seen is an electric screen. Poultry farmers use them to keep foxes away. Basically it's a panel about the size of a sprung single-bed base. The old type, electrified by way of a built-in battery. You need to wear protective rubber gloves when you're handling it so you don't get a wallop. But I shot the fucker instead. Nah, I rarely carry a gun. Guns are against the law. The tongue in that cellophane bag Picasso carried in his tool bag and Winters taking Greg Swags's German shepherd had got me thinking I'd come up against a dog. I tossed in a piece of meat laced with dope I'd bought from a vet.

'There, girl, eat that.' Five minutes and it was dreaming it'd found the biggest bone in the world.

I went in, stepped over it and had a look upstairs. Other than a darkroom, which contained no photographs, it was just bedrooms. Nothing worth telling you about, except that in the downstairs living room there was a framed photo of him on a horse. Which clinched what I had in mind for him. The last thing I needed was a killer who was afraid of horses.

A door to a flight of stone stairs that led down to a basement was open. If Lucille was still in one piece, she had to be in it. Which meant I couldn't let her see me. She'd know someone was about though: as soon as I hit the halfway mark, more dogs started snarling. They sensed I wasn't their owner, and she must have too, because she started calling out: 'Hello, hello, help me,' all that. I think I got her hopes up.

I came straight back out. I'd only brought enough meat for one dog. She was alive. Knowing that would do for now. As I say, there's always an extra angle if you go looking for it. And like all angles, some people don't see them. But I'm not some people. I'd found one, and, with any luck, it would allow me to deal with my family and get this whole thing with Chilly Winters arresting his daughter for it over and done with. And the upshot of that would be that Greg would be released. Everybody happy. Except Lucille and the Donavans of course. Still, you can't please everyone.

I was going to make good use of Picasso at the riding stables is what I'm saying.

So I went out there. It was a Thursday night, and I knew that on Saturday night my sister Amy would be out dancing, usually in the village hall, though that shindig she'd been talking to Cormac about would do just as nicely. It sounded as if it was further away, a bigger outing than usual – in Dublin maybe. She'd be home even later then. I'd already picked up what I needed so I went for it.

That prize-winning mare of Anne's was in a field behind Amy and Edna's cottage. I parked along the road and walked up Conor's drive with a bucket of feed nuts. I'd mixed follicle-inducing stimulants with them. The mare came over when I shook the bucket. I leaned in through the fence, tipped it out on the grass and stood back. She got tucked in.

I did exactly the same the following night. Then the next morning I was back at Picasso's. Again he stayed home all day, until about eight o'clock, when he drove off in his Transit.

I went in, same story with his bitch (doped her) – only this time I'd brought a little something for him. A surveillance laptop with a built-in phone – though not the one he'd appeared on – a riding crop, a horse's hood and a bee-keeper's outfit.

Then I went downstairs.

The dogs weren't the only ones making noise: such a clamour. A kind of frantic rustling. It had to be coming from Lucille's cell. There were four cells running along a corridor at the bottom of the steps. The first two were open; the others were bolted shut.

This time there could be no mistake. She would definitely know that someone other than Picasso was down there with her.

She'd hear me as I crept past her cell, under the hatch so she wouldn't see me, to the fourth, where the dogs were. It had an internal door.

This time she really called out. Never stopped. 'Hello, please help me,' crying and begging. Sorry, Lucille, I haven't come this far to be put off now. I'd ignored her crying when she was a baby, and I could ignore it again.

So Picasso had his own private little jail. Wonder what kind of warden he was. There were a few more bone crunchers to contend with. I fed them what Sleeping Beauty upstairs was dreaming on, and checked the first two cells while they dozed off.

Each of the cells contained a big wooden crate the size of a coffin. The timber on the inside of the one I lifted had been gnawed. The bottom was caked in shit, matted with black hairs. I heard squealing and scratching below my feet, coming from under the flagstones. Rats they sounded like. So that's what I'd been hearing rustling in Lucille's cell. Wouldn't fancy doing time in there.

I went into the dogs' cell, stepped over them and opened the door that led down a flight of wooden steps into an artist's studio. Recreational activities for the inmates – I didn't think so. What a carry-on. I'd never seen anything like it. Human hands in the freezer in

142

case he felt peckish, a dog's tongue in frozen saliva. So I was right about that. It was the one he took with him when he didn't feel like walking the rest of it.

The second room was a gallery. I'm no connoisseur, but I'd've given odds no art expert had ever seen paintings like his before.

The bones in the dogs' cell more or less confirmed how his victims were paid in return for sitting for him. I'll leave that to your imagination. If you haven't worked it out, you haven't got any. Let's just say the inmates who had literally given him a hand were no longer in residence, and I doubt they'd been paroled. Every enterprise has its little waste-disposal problems. Saved him digging graves and buying dog food.

Not that I'd ask him to confirm that. Though I did have questions for him.

After I'd made sure that Anne's mare had reacted to those follicle-inducing stimulants, I was going to invite Picasso out to meet the family. The wonders of modern technology. I'd a spot of email in mind for him when he came back. That's why I'd left him the laptop, logged on to the internet and ready to go. A slow way of communicating but effective. I could've rung him of course, but this had a better angle to it. Either way, he'd know that if he didn't do what he was told, Chilly Winters'd be asking him if he had a licence to run his own private prison.

LUCILLE

If I was ever to see my mother again, I had to put the fear of Picasso catching me trying to escape out of my mind. But it wasn't easy. Others' lives would be at risk. I would see to that. He would force me to.

I had read in his journal that he'd been told about Gemma and me by Lisa Shine and Jackie Hay. If he could break their will, he could break mine. And the thought of informing on people I knew was more than I could bear. But I could feel myself becoming weaker. And I was afraid to sleep.

The rat in my cell had finished eating the other one. While I was awake, it stayed in its corner watching me. But when exhaustion set in, it seemed to know that it was safe to come out. I had already woken to find it sitting on my chest, staring at me. I'd bounced up and sent it scurrying. Picasso had been standing looking in through the peephole. The ones in the crate may have been his way of letting me know that I would eventually wake to find myself covered with them. The single one though was used in a far cleverer way. It was also there to keep me awake. If I slept, what would hunger force it to do? Without proper food and rest, I would begin to hallucinate. In that state, I would give him the names he wanted. I wouldn't be able to help myself.

Because I didn't know when it was morning or when it was night, I couldn't tell when there was no sound of movement in the floor above, whether he had gone out or to bed. But I could tell when it was time for him to exercise his dogs. He used to take them out several at a time. They seemed to know when he was on his way and would whine. And while they were gone, I worked on as fast as I could.

I'd scored my way through the ceiling and removed a square of plaster and lath, big enough for me to squeeze up through the joists. But first I'd need to remove the same area of floor directly above. By hammering my one and only nail through the boards, then pulling it back out with the claw, I was able to make a hole. I'd straighten the nail and make another one next to it. By perforating a square outline of the floorboards I could eventually cut my way through. I could only pray that I was working on a section of flooring that was covered by a piece of furniture, to avoid Picasso discovering what I was up to from above.

And then, after about an hour or so, when I'd managed to penetrate about four inches along a line where the joist met the underside of the floor, I heard someone coming down the stairs. The remaining dogs started snarling. They didn't do that when Picasso came down. It had to be somebody else. Whoever it was, he wouldn't help me. I pleaded with him, but he just ignored me. Then the dogs went silent. He went into their cell and down to the rooms below. Then he left. But it was the way he'd come and gone. He'd crept under the serving hatch in my cell door. He didn't want me to see him. Why? Why didn't he help me?

When Picasso returned he came running down the stairs shouting my name, 'Lucille? Lucille?' as though he'd expected to find me gone. When he saw me through the hatch, he stood back and composed himself. Other than the time I'd told him about the computer, I'd never seen him lose control. It was the most unnerving thing about him. He was always so polite, so unruffled. In some respects he reminded me of a doctor discussing with a group of interns how to dissect a human body for medical reasons, dispassionately and matter-of-factly. He had done horrible, horrible things, yet he seemed removed from the fact that he done them to living people. It was almost as if he was referring to something as trivial as the weather.

'I see we have had a visitor, Lucille.'

'Yes.'

'Yet you are still here. His motivation clearly does not extend to your freedom. You require another replacement timber?'

'I have nothing to trade with.'

'He did not speak to you?'

'A glimpse of the back of a pair of corduroy trousers and men's shoes are all that suggests he even is a he.'

'You did not see his face?'

146

'He didn't show it.'

'Then he has a reason for keeping it hidden. Strange, since identifying him at a later date would depend on your liberty. He *is* cautious. Ted Lyle?'

'Maybe.'

'I shall make inquiries.'

'I thought you had.'

'Mr Lyle has not been at home of late.'

A mobile phone rang upstairs.

'Would you excuse me?'

With any luck, he was being called out. I could get back to my 'motivation'. Which clearly did extend to my freedom.

RED DOCK

You should've seen Picasso's face when he saw what was on that laptop.

Here he was: 'Aagh. Aagh.' I thought he was gonna have a heart attack. He was watching himself killing Gemma. Thought I'd treat him to a spot of home entertainment. I don't think Picasso should watch himself killing people on laptops. It's bad for his nerves. He should go and see a doctor about it.

Did you ever see those old films based on Greek mythology? Where one of the goddesses fights her corner and Zeus fights his, and somebody who has offended the gods has to be snuffed out. 'Release the Kraken,' Zeus commands, and everybody goes 'Aagh!' as this big dinosaur-type crocodile comes up out of the sea and licks its lips at the sight of this poor virgin who's been bound to a cliff to be gobbled up. Must have been handy having your own Kraken to get shot of people.

Well Picasso was gonna be mine. Release Picasso! In Clonkeelin.

Now for the plan I had in mind to work, I had to see to it that the laptop I was using, not the one I'd left in Picasso's, would eventually land in Chilly Winters' lap. And I had to make Winters believe that it wasn't me but his daughter who had been communicating with Picasso. And she had to appear to be in control, not intimidated by him, relaxed, casual. Why? Because relaxed casual threats from the right quarters are far more intimidating than giving your opponent the impression that you fear him. That weakens threats. In this instance, forget all that crap about women being frightened by killers. I had to make Winters believe that Lucille had the power to frighten Picasso more than the other way round, through the information she held on him, and her use of what she would believe to be her anonymity being preserved via modern technology. This *is* the information-technology age.

'Good evening, Cornelius,' I typed. 'And how are you?' Spot of informality there for me old mate Picasso. I like that. It fits in with the 'casual threats' approach. Just because you can put a guy away and ruin his life doesn't mean you can't be friendly.

He looked around him as if somehow he was going to see where I was.

'You can speak,' I typed. 'I can both hear and see you.'

He peered into the camera I'd connected to the top of the upright lid as if he expected me to peer back at him. In close-up like this it hit me again that I knew him from somewhere, but I just couldn't place him.

Nah. I already had him. I'd seen letters addressed to him on his sideboard during my first visit. Cornelius Hockler. Faces might change a little over the years but names don't. And who could fail to recognise a name like that? Me and old Corn went way back.

Anyway, 'Sit down and be comfortable,' I typed.

He pulled up a chair.

'That's better. Nice and comfy?'

Here he was: 'Yes, yes,' nodding away at the same time. I'd say he was more surprised by that laptop than his victims had been by him.

'Who … who are you?' he asked.

'A benefactor.'

'A benefactor?'

'Yes, Cornelius. I want you to work for me.'

'Me? Work for you? In what capacity?'

'In your field of expertise.'

That one threw him. 'You wish me to paint for you?'

'Your other field.'

'My *other* field?'

'Now don't be modest, Cornelius. Think of the Irish word for church.'

'I'm afraid Irish was not one of my subjects.'

'It begins with a "K".'

He considered it long enough to say, 'K … k … k …?' then shook his head. I thought he was gonna come out with 'Ku Klux Klan' for a minute.

'I'll give you a clue. Sick: three letters, then front it with a "K".'

A big deep-thought face showed up. 'Sick, three

letters … ill … ill … *kill* … You want me to *kill* for you?'

'Don't look so shocked, Cornelius. Right now you're doing it for free.'

'You wish me to become an *assassin*?'

'That's one way of seeing it.'

He was seeing it another way, the crafty bastard. Gone was the musing and the deep thought. Now he was arching an eyebrow, the way people do when a big opportunity has just turned up.

Here he was: 'A *paid* assassin?'

Fuck me, the cunt was looking for a backhander. Which threw me. I hadn't expected it. I'd expected him to be biting his nails. Why was he asking me that? Maybe he was after a job. Whatever it was, he interpreted my silence for what it was – I was weighing up what he'd said.

Then he put a head on it. 'Would there be … a …' he said. I could smell that something else was on the way. But not '… a possibility of a small advance?'

A small fucking advance? The gall of the bastard. This guy had an odd way of treating blackmailers.

'You appreciate, Cornelius – "Cornelius", such a lovely name—'

'Thank you.'

'—that I can *persuade* you to work for me.'

'So I have observed.'

'And that a copy of this evidence will find its way to the law if anything should ever happen to me.'

'Please do not forget to take your vitamins.'

151

He always had a sense of humour. 'So we have an understanding?'

'Male or female?'

'Who?'

'Your difficulties?'

Amy and Edna Donavan were first in line. I began with them.

'Female.'

'Pretty?'

Pretty? What was he after – girls to paint? 'Not especially. Why?'

'Age?'

'Fifties.'

'Oh, I couldn't, I couldn't. I couldn't countenance ladies of an advanced age. I just couldn't.'

'Fifty's not advanced.'

'Quite. But my models are always much younger.'

That's all I needed – a fussy serial killer. 'The victims' gender and ages are neither here nor there. They won't be modelling for you.'

'And the riding crop?' (The one I'd left beside the laptop.)

'Bring it and the other gear with you.'

'To where?'

'Clonkeelin.'

'Why?'

'Instructions will arrive in a minute. Study them on your way over. You'll have thirty minutes. Don't let me down.'

Well, well, well, whaddayaknow. That's my big word for the day. So Corn was coming to work for me.

Corn wasn't a bad old boy, as it happens. Come to think of it, he was a bad *old boy*. Me and him used to share the same dormitory. The size of him should've given him away sooner. He was always a lanky bastard. Mind you, like myself, he'd put on a bit of weight since then.

Hope he isn't afraid of wasps.

LUCILLE

'I must confess, Lucille, the powers of connivance at work here have surprised even me.'

'What powers of connivance?'

'Your mother's or your grandfather's perhaps.'

'I don't understand.'

'You were correct, it seems. You told no one you were staying in Clonkeelin—'

'No one.'

'But you did. Your family. You are related to Amy and Edna Donavan?'

'They're my mother's aunts. Why?'

'Your grandfather's sisters?'

'Yes.'

'He would benefit from their passing?'

'Benefit from their *passing*?'

'Since no one in Dublin knew of the Donavans, then no one from Dublin would have known where to locate your laptop. Logical?'

'Yes, but—'

'Then it follows that someone *in* Clonkeelin took it.

And since my own liberty now depends on the demise of your mother's two aunts, I can only surmise that the communication I have just received can only have come *from* Clonkeelin. Such is my reading. Time is pressing. Anon.'

It was madness. I couldn't take it in. Picasso was telling me that he was being forced to kill my two great-aunts and that my grandfather was the only one with motive.

I couldn't even begin to understand it. And he was gone. I could do nothing to stop him. Even if I could have smashed my way through to the upstairs room, I would have been too late.

RED DOCK

OK, I'd always intended to pull this next part off by myself. The only problem I had with it was it involved lifting. And, as I say, I avoid anything that involves lifting, if I can. Then Corn came along.

When it was over, it had to look like three deaths had occurred through sheer bad luck. Crime couldn't come into it. The fourth death, Anne Donavan's, would be put down to Picasso. That's how Chilly Winters would initially see it. He'd have already linked right into the unlikely coincidence of Picasso just happening to strike the same night three others had died on the same farm. Who could miss it? Then Winters'd discover what else I was gonna leave for him. He'd know the truth, or what he thought was the truth: that Lucille was behind it, but that she had connived to cover it up so she could get her hands on what the Donavans had.

As I say, because I'd had over twenty years to study the Donavans' habits, I knew what all four did from week to week. Amy's love of dancing; Edna, who sat stuffing herself every night in front of the TV and rarely went to bed before one; their nights at bingo; Conor's weekly card game, his involvement with the Irish Horse Board, a divorcee he kept company on Saturday nights; Anne, who ran a horse riding business, and attended shows, showing her mare ...

They say actors should never work with animals or kids. Well, it's a load of crap as far as scams are concerned. The plan I'd perfected had not only begun with a kid, it was to continue with Anne's mare and a bull.

And since I'd already kicked it off by feeding Anne's mare a couple of times, when all the Donavans were safely tucked up in their scratchers, I was now lining up for the net with my old mate Corn. Appropriate name for what goes on down on the farm.

Thirty-five minutes after I'd emailed him, I watched his Transit drive past the entrance to the riding stables. He parked farther along the road and walked back. From behind a hedge at the other end of the field, with a pair of night-vision goggles, I saw him enter the field and go over to the mare. She was nudging a foal. It was lying flat out on the grass. He picked it up, carried it over to a drainage ditch, the mare tailing after him, put it down, got into the ditch and lifted it in. Then he went across to the cottage, leaving her standing peering into the ditch, snorting and prodding the way horses do when some fucker's just dumped their kid in a dark and dingy ditch.

So far he'd carried out my instructions perfectly.

Now in preparation for this over the years, which included finding out a lot about horses, my problem was how the fuck do you make a mare foal when you want her to? Well, the answer is you can't. Nature's nature and that's all there is to it. Then again, maternity wards bring women on all the time. They bypass nature. The truth of this was that if the mare didn't cooperate, then it was simply back to plan B, then C, D, E and all the rest of them. I'd an alphabetful. But the way I'd worked this particular one out was based on something that happened to me when I was a kid.

Horses carry for eleven months and one week, and foals born five or six weeks premature rarely survive – something to do with their lungs forming during the last weeks of gestation according to my vet book. In other words, they're born with hardly any lungs. Which got me thinking.

When I left that home, I'd nowhere to go. I slept in containers in the docks, used the wash-and-brush-up facilities public toilets had in those days and got a job in a rag-and-bone yard, cash in hand, four quid a week, on the north side of the city centre, the working-class area.

Men used to rent a handcart for ten bob a day (that's fifty pence to you younger ones). They were the two-wheel type you had to push. Stick yourself between the shafts and sweat your bollocks off. You could rent a pony to pull it for a quid a day. Most men pushed. They'd buy a basket of delft, go round the houses – 'Any rags? Scrap iron?' – and give maybe a cup in exchange for a few woollens or an old fire grate – anything they could weigh in. Some men rented carts and went down the docks and bought a load of herrings and flogged them round the streets at a shilling a dozen; fruit and veg was another one – and bags of coal. I'm talking about men who were signing on the dole and doing the double.

Because there was no grass in this area – there wasn't a garden within a mile, let alone a field, just streets of terraced houses with no bathrooms – horses were given a nosebag: oats mainly, hay rarely.

But the thing I remember most were the horses' stomachs. It used to amaze me that such big strong animals could be so weak in the stomach. Horses can't throw up the way you and I can. The kind of gut-ache they get can often lead to colic. It makes them sweat and they keep looking back at their flanks where the pain is – their intestines have twisted and they're wondering what the fuck's going on. A fine healthy specimen can go down and not get up again and be dead within two hours.

There are different types of colic, and without going into it in detail the horses round what I soon began to call 'our way' – mainly because the people were friendly and made me feel like one of them – sometimes got colic, because they'd eaten their straw bed or had been fed too quickly after building up a sweat between the shafts. To regulate their diet, the old guy I worked for used to send me up to the graveyard to get a sackful of grass. I'd no shears or anything. I had to pull it out by the roots. Sometimes, if you were lucky, they'd just mown between the graves and you could grab that.

Though if old Francie McArdle had known, he'd have given me a boot in the arse. Diesel from the mower on the grass wasn't any good for horses either, y'see. Sensitive bastards.

Francie was a thieving old goat, by the way. He was loaded, though to look at him you'd think he hadn't tuppence. He used to wear an old fawn overcoat tied round his waist with a length of rope. If you stole lead off a roof and threw it on his scales – the old low flatbed type I'm talking about – he'd stick his shin against the bed to stop it going down as far as it should so it would register less weight and you'd get less money than you were entitled to. He'd strike up some interesting conversation or crack a joke, thinking you weren't wise.

'Get away t'fuck, ya aul' bollocks ye,' I'd've hit him with. My accent was a bit thicker in those days and not that of the suave sophisticate before you today.

He ended up having to let me go. Some fucker set fire to his yard one night when he was well stocked with rags and the whole lot went up.

The reason I'm telling you all this is because when I went and saw the state of McArdle's yard – carts burned and all that – I wondered where the horses were. And I asked Francie. I was really only interested in one of them: a white pony mare called Peggy. She was in foal and I'd wanted to see it being born.

'She lost it, Red,' he said.

'Whaddaya mean?'

'She took fright and it brought her on early.'

'Where is she now?'

'Sure I'd nowhere t'keep her, Red.'

He'd sold her to the knacker man for dog meat. She was getting on. That's why he had her in foal. He wanted a replacement out of her before she copped it. The rest went to tinkers.

And this experience got me thinking. If fear could bring a mare on, was there any other way to make her foal before her time? So I looked into it. A vet book told me that by mixing follicle-inducing stimulants in with a mare's feed, you could bring her into season quicker, for covering, but that you had to be sure you didn't let a mare who was already in foal eat the same feed, otherwise she'd give birth prematurely – within forty-eight hours usually – but the foal would die. Because of that lung thing, y'know, it wouldn't have a breath. Horses need breath. Bit of technical info for you there.

So I'm saying to myself: Conor's a stallion man. He'd have a supply of stimulants. Lucille had gone to Clonkeelin. It doesn't take a genius – after the event – to see that she could have got access to them. What if I stuff Anne's mare with stimulants? All you have to do is shake a bucket and she'll come over, tip them out and away you go, leaving her to it. And since mares invariably wait for the cover of darkness before foaling – gut-instinct survival crap that's in them going back to the days when predators were knocking about and would've eaten the foal – the chances are she'll do the same.

So I went back out to see how my bucket had worked, night three, Saturday, and found her lying on her side.

And because the Donavans had no reason to be keeping a strict eye on her, because she wasn't due for nearly six weeks, I more or less had a free hand.

Anyway, she got to her feet when she saw me coming, and I shone a torch on her rear end and saw that her croup had dropped – the croup is the part between the top of the rump and the tail. When it loses its roundness and slackens into a slightly concaved state, it's a sign that the muscles around her birth canal are relaxing to enable the passage of the foal. She started nudging her flanks with her nose. The pain of coming into labour makes a mare do that and stand with her legs stretched out, like a rocking horse. Her waters had burst and the membrane covering the foal's hoof was showing.

I left her to it and went back to the driveway: horses can get nervous with strangers around and hold off until they've gone. Half an hour later she went down, and I saw her continually looking back at her rear end and heaving. I went along behind the hedge of the adjoining field and had a closer look. The foal was on its way. Two tiny hooves had emerged, and I saw the membrane covering its snout being sucked in and out over its nostrils as it fought for air. Then its little head came forward, and the mare got to her feet. On average, foaling from this point usually lasts about fifteen minutes, with the mare getting up and down, until the widest part – the shoulders – emerge, then the rest comes much more easily.

When the mare was down, and with junior halfway

out, I climbed through the fence and clipped a lunge lead to her halter. We were in business. All I had to do was arrange for the foal to fall into a six-foot-deep drainage ditch. A drainage ditch, for you city folk, is a trench that runs round the edge of a field. In winter when the ground is constantly wet, the rain drains into it through perforated pipes just below the topsoil. Drier land means better grass and fewer rushes. As far as my use of it was concerned, well it's like this: because I'd studied this for so long, and because the law had first to see this not as a deliberate killing – make that killings – I'd been teaching myself all about life down on the farm.

And if you're gonna arrange deaths that don't have foul play stamped on them, use what the person does on a daily basis. That's the conclusion I'd come to. In this case, farming books will tell you how to avoid fatalities. By reversing the process, they tell you how to bring them about.

This, for instance, was based on a farmer whose mare was due to foal. He went down in the middle of the night to see how she was getting on and found her flat out with her rear end hanging over a ditch, foaling. Being a dumb animal, she wasn't able to tell what she was doing. The foal literally passed out of her and went 'bonk' into the ditch. The farmer went in to rescue it, and dumbo, all worried because she couldn't see her baby, in a rush to get to her feet, back-kicked him, tried to go in and save junior and squashed her owner to death. It didn't say whether Chilly Winters took her hoofprints and got her twenty years. Tragic, I know. But that's the way it goes.

And Picasso was rapping Edna's door. As per the instructions I'd emailed his laptop. He knew where to go and what to do. No detail was overlooked. I'd even included a few suggestions on how to get her to cooperate, plus info about her and their vet. The dialogue was his own. I was standing behind a hedge at the front of the cottage in my capacity as official observer.

She was in front of the TV with a fag in her mouth and her rollers in. She opened the window.

'Good evening,' he said. 'So sorry to bother you. Might your name be Edna Donavan?'

'It is, yes.'

'Well, in that case, Amy sent me for you.'

'Amy?'

'Amy is the name I was given. I was fishing the river then making my way across the field when a lady of that name, tending a mare, called me, and here I am. I'll be more than pleased to take you to her. I have to go back for my rod in any event.'

'This is all very strange.'

'Apropos?'

'Eh?'

Yeah, it was definitely his own dialogue. I don't remember including any apropos.

'What's she doing with the mare this time o' night and her away to the dance?'

'There's a man called Cormac with her. He appears

to have hurt his leg. Amy mentioned that you had nursing experience and may be of assistance.'

Homework. It's the only way to get away with anything. Edna used to work in the General.

'I'll get my coat,' she said. She also put on her wellingtons and Picasso shone a torch and led the way. I traipsed along behind a hedge for scene three.

The mare was still peering into the ditch and snorting when they reached her, and Edna took it by its halter and went to soothe it. 'There, girl, there,' she said, trying to calm her, and at the same reminding Picasso what he'd said about Amy and Cormac. 'Where are they?'

'In there, madam.'

'Where?'

'There.'

I couldn't see the bottom of the ditch, but when he pushed her she had to have landed straight on top of the foal. And she must've been eighteen stone. No newborn could've survived that, lungs or no lungs.

The mare started getting into an even bigger state over her foal and Picasso tried to lead her away. But she wouldn't follow. She kept straining at the neck into the ditch.

So he clipped away under her girth with the crop to get her going and led her down into the ditch, jumping back up onto the grass as he trotted her along it towards where Edna was lying.

But the mare stopped. I heard Edna wailing, 'Oh my God. In the name of God,' and generally making it known that she wasn't too keen on Picasso's equestrian activities. He had to shut her up. They were behind a hedge and couldn't be seen from the road, but with the mare going mad and Edna going mad and her rollers coming undone, a farmer out tending stock might've heard. As might Anne Donavan, who was up at the house watching TV. Conor himself was with his fancy piece and wouldn't be back till later. But there was still too much noise.

Picasso slipped a hood over the mare's head so she couldn't see, then, with the riding crop, laid into her rear end, which was sensitive from having just given birth. What could she do but bolt forward on top of Edna?

That Picasso's a fucking eejit. He kept apologising to the dumb bastard every time he hit it. 'Oh I'm so sorry, my darling, I'm so sorry.' Fuck's sake.

She backed up then reared on her hind legs, and he apologised again with the crop, and it sent her hinds forward enough to ensure that when she brought her forelegs down, they hit the spot. Which shut Ed up. But was she dead? He couldn't tell without getting in himself and checking. Dodgy. The mare might have done the same to him. A mother, head away, protecting her young – not recommended. I always advise people to stay away from mad mares who're protecting their young.

Though he did need to give Edna a couple more goes to make sure.

He got on the mare's back. Risky. That trench was

up to her withers and only a few feet wide. She could cripple him. Still, the photograph on his living-room wall said his arse had been on a horse before; he obviously knew what he was doing. He fed the lunge lead through her mouth and, using it like a bit and reins, backed her up then kicked her onto Ed and junior. Hard going with all that bucking and screeching. Difficult to be accurate.

Then she reared and when her fores landed I heard a crack.

I doubt there was a roller in place. My guess was he'd give her one more go for luck, and that did it. Difficult one to call – how many times you need to trample an eighteen-stone woman with a one-ton mare to do the trick. Having administered a final trot or two, that was him for the night, as far as riding without a safety helmet was concerned. He went across to the cowshed.

I went and shone my trusty torch and had a look at how Edna was managing. When the light hit her face, I thought I was looking at a Halloween mask. Bye, sis.

But was the damage consistent with this type of … 'misadventure'? How the fuck should I know? Who's to say how much trampling a mare would be capable of when trying to save its foal? That's how this would look – should, anyway – to the law. For a while. Until they realised Lucille had orchestrated it, as I've said.

As for the foal itself, I could now see that he hadn't thrown Edna on top of it. I think that Picasso's a bit of an animal lover. It still looked dead though. The mare was nudging it but it wasn't moving.

Now, as you know, one of the most important ingredients in farming comes from cows. Then farmers spread it to make the grass grow. Years ago a man might've had an old byre in which to shelter his livestock over the winter months; today it's intensive state-of-the-art slatted sheds – barns with slatted flooring, each with a centre aisle between two holding bays. Cattle are taken off the land at the back end of the year when the grass has stopped growing and kept in a shed where they eat silage, which is grass cut in spring or summer, rolled into a four-foot bale and wrapped in black bin-liner-type plastic. You must've seen them in fields; they look like giant snooker balls from a distance. The grass gradually breaks down, ferments you might say, in the plastic, which gives it a high acid content. It's not only good for fattening cattle; it also makes it easier for the farmer to look after them. Once eaten, the silage passes through their systems and comes out the other end as slurry then falls down through the slats they're standing on into a man-made pit the size of a swimming pool – effectively we're talking about a swimming pool of liquid cow shit. Then comes spring, the cattle are let back onto the land and some of the slats are removed to allow a pipe from a slurry spreader to be lowered down into it so it can be sucked up and sprayed over the land as fertiliser. All very recyclable, and all very boring.

Unless you have an alternative use for it.

Poisonous gas builds up in this slurry. Methane. And that's when it becomes interesting. Which is why I chose it. They'd removed the slats for the slurry man to come and empty the pit. Every year they did this. And they'd brought their bull in.

He'd been out all winter. But his ladies were out grazing. And he didn't like that. He was keen to earn his pay, wanted to be out playing with them. Which meant he was in a bad mood – and that made him dangerous. Horny bulls kill ten men in Ireland every year. More in a good year.

This one was in the left-hand-side holding bay. Picasso was shaking a bucket of beef nuts beside him to let him smell them. He put the bucket in the opposite holding bay, opened the bull's gate, got the fuck out of the way, watched the bull cross over to the holding bay opposite and get tucked into the nuts then went back up and closed the gate, locking the bull in the bay where the slats had been removed.

Oh, just in case you're wondering why I'd chosen Amy for this, instead of Edna, well Edna was too fat, y'see. Amy was only a skinny little thing – about seven stone. Whoever removed those slats removed only enough for Amy to fall through. For Edna, a few more would have to have been taken out – a job for two men. Also, if need be, Picasso could carry Amy over to the slats and drop her down through them into the pit, whereas he would never have managed Ed. He'd have had to drag her and that would leave marks. I had to credit Lucille, in the law's eyes, with the cop on to think of these things.

I saw headlights pulling in at the front of the cottage.

Amy had come home from the dance to put her feet up. But there was one waltz yet to go. Or shall I call it a tango? With the bull.

Picasso put on his bee-keeper's gear, overalls, gloves and a veil – he didn't look like a blushing bride in it – and came up to the top of the centre aisle where someone had brought in jumping poles to paint. They stood upright against the wall. To their left was a wasps' nest.

For this to work, y'see, the law'd have to at first con-clude that Amy came home, saw the TV on, wondered where her sister was, saw the light on in the shed, went in to check, found that the bull was loose and in the wrong bay, tried to shoo it back to where it should have been – out of harm's way from the open slats – and found that it, coming into the mating season and pissed off, ran at her, hit the pole and broke open the nest. The wasps went mad and started stinging all round them, which sent the bull nuts and he chased Amy, who couldn't see too well with all the wasps stinging her eyes, fell into the pit and was poisoned by the gas – it acts in seconds.

So Picasso took hold of a pole and cracked open the nest. Then he bolted for the door and left the wasps to blame the bull. I wasn't sure about this bit. I didn't know how wasps blamed bulls. Could they sting through hide for instance? Leather's tough. Then again, hide gets a good deal of its toughness only in the tanning process. Besides, it had two eyes, two nostrils, a mouth, open ears and balls the size of milk bottles to sting. How the

170

latter's performance might later be affected, I wasn't sure of either. I've never performed with my nuts covered in wasp stings, so I can't say.

By the time I'd crept round from my ringside seat – a hole high up in the cowshed wall where a block had been left out for ventilation – (I'd covered it with a little mesh to keep the stingers at bay) – Picasso had removed his veil, gone over to the cottage, rapped on the door and was talking to Amy through the open living-room window.

'Excuse me,' he was saying. 'Might your name be Amy?'

'Yes. And you are?'

'I am with the vet: Mr Feeney.'

'What's Feeney doing here?'

'Administering to the bull. It has slipped its moorings, so to speak, and has injured itself as a result. Your sister Edna is asking for you.'

'Edna's asking for me? I thought she was in bed.'

'She may well have been. Now she is in the slatted cowshed with the vet.'

'What does she want me for?'

'She is of the opinion that you are the one who normally deals with the bull.'

'Why didn't she come herself? Why did she send you?'

'I volunteered. Would you like me to fetch her?'

'No, it's all right. I'd better come.'

She opened the door and followed him round behind the cottage and halfway across the yard then stopped at the noise coming from inside the shed. The bull was wrecking the place.

'Is he loose?'

'He is. Though he presents no immediate danger.'

'What's all that buzzing?'

'Perhaps the vet has his electric shaver on. To shave around the wound before stitching.'

'What – with him going buck mad?'

'He's waiting until the anaesthetic takes effect.'

'Where's his van?'

'We drove it straight in and locked the doors in case the bull got out.'

'Oh.' Talkative bitch – I thought she was never gonna shut up. 'I'd be afraid to go any further with all that commotion. I've never heard him this bad. Edna?'

'I doubt she will hear you.'

She saw Picasso's bee-keeper's veil lying near the wicker door. 'What's that?'

He got it and put it on. She didn't fancy him in it. And no way was she going anywhere near that door.

'This?'

'Yes. What's it for?'

Fuck knows what she thought with him standing there in that get-up. He looked like something out of a sci-fi movie. She made to back away and Picasso scooped her into his arms.

I didn't like it. A bull charging her down would not leave paw marks on her. A small point, I know. But if forensic found bruises consistent with being grabbed, it might ruin everything. Still, what was I worrying about? Lucille would get the blame when the time came.

Picasso opened the wicker and turfed her in then went in after her.

And I returned to my air vent. Amy was standing screaming and grabbing her hair as the wasps got to work. Picasso lifted her over the metal feeder into the bay where the bull was going mad. Then he stepped back.

To be fair to her, she didn't faint. She just stood in the corner wailing. She didn't try to climb back out either. Whether she was in too much of a state or she knew Picasso would prevent her, I couldn't say. The wasps were keeping her mind on other things.

The strange thing was the bull never charged. I thought he'd be so out of his head that he would've gone straight for her. Maybe she'd been good to him. You can never plan for how an animal will react.

Picasso climbed over, lifted her into the aisle then carried her up and turfed her back over the feeder rail to where the bull was.

The bull was bucking so much he couldn't help but ram her. He bucked all round him, caught her with a rear hind in the small of her back and bolted for the opposite end of the bay as she slid down the wall. The methane in the silage'd finish her off.

Picasso went in and dropped her through the opening in the slats. Then he opened the gate to let the animal have the run of the place. There was no need for him to stay behind and check that the fumes'd finish her off.

Everybody needs oxygen and there wasn't any down there.

She didn't try to climb back out. I couldn't hear her spluttering as the slurry covered her face. The bull was making too much noise for that.

I went to my car, emailed Picasso's laptop in his Transit (I'd told him to bring it with him), telling him what to do next: see to Conor then Anne. Job done.

All the Donavans would be gone.

And I would have what I had wanted since I was nine years old.

PICASSO

It was now clear that I was at the mercy of a devious and savage mind. Under penalty of exposure, I had been blackmailed into dispatching two sisters in a fashion both prolonged and unnecessary. I have little time for gratuitous violence. It is the preserve of the sadist. Having to treat two harmless creatures in such a manner was very distressing. I shall not describe it to you in detail, but I have never experienced anything like it.

However, while I had initially considered the tenuous possibility that the only person in a position to exert such control over my actions might have been Conor Donavan, it soon became evident that this was not the case. Another's deception was at work. But who was this unknown person? Naturally I had deduced that he, or she, in some way had an association with those now departed. Perhaps a relative, conspiring to profit from their demise by way of a bequest or suchlike. A precise identification was required, and it was towards this goal that I had taken my own investigative measures.

You will recall that I had taken possession of Jackie Hay's camcorder. If a camera had placed me in this predicament then a camera might steer a course back out of it. I had therefore placed the camcorder on the dashboard of my Transit before the incident to which I have just alluded.

Consequently I now had footage of a man coming out through the entrance to the riding stables. Darkness, alas, had been against me. His identity remained a mystery. However all mysteries provide clues. And while I may not have been able to discern his face, he did have one distinguishing characteristic.

'Lucille, do any of your male relatives walk with a limp?'

'Wha ...?'

'Do you *know* anyone with a limp?'

'No.'

The Donavan sisters' funeral might provide the answers I was seeking. If the man on the film *was* a relative, his gait would single him out from the cortège.

Of course to take this a measure further, there was my own position to consider. Weak, yes, but strong also. Whatever the nature of his involvement, I had been instrumental, and, indeed, it had been made abundantly clear was to be of further assistance in bringing his as-yet-unknown aim to fruition. If profit it be then surely I was deserving of my rightful share, as it were, of the take. After all, had not his evidence against me been rendered somewhat academic? I now had similarly damaging evidence against him. Were I to be apprehended, police analysis equipment would enhance his image. If he continued to blackmail me, I could counter by threatening reciprocity. He could not turn me in any more than I him. Any further participation on my part, therefore – participation, I might add, which had already been requested, but which I had had occasion to withhold – would have to be remunerated. Fair's fair.

'My apologies, Lucille, for having cast aspersions on your grandfather.'

'My grandfather?'

'He is not responsible for the deaths of your great-aunts, because he and your mother are to meet a similar fate.'

'Oh God, please don't harm my mother, please ... I'll do anything you say. Please ...'

Lucille had undergone a rather distressing experience and was in a state of shock. Had I not returned when I did and dispersed the rats with a blazing torch, she might not have survived.

The rats had eaten their way through the crate. Her weight on a makeshift ladder she had constructed had made the wood cave in, smashing the timber they'd been gnawing through. She had done it to herself. She had been so determined to break out through the ceiling that she hadn't noticed until it was too late, and I found them biting into her. She had tried to climb up this ladder to get away from them, to get a hold on the small opening she had made in the floorboards so she could hang from the ceiling, but they had jumped up onto her, and she couldn't shake them off. Clinging onto her clothes in such numbers, their weight brought her back down. She was covered in a feeding frenzy of teeth. When she screamed they went for her open mouth. They tore at her hair, her dress ... there were too many to fend off. When she tried they went straight for her face. When she covered her face, the rest of her was exposed. They were between her legs, under her arms, locking their jaws into her fingers to get at her eyes ...

I had placed her in the adjoining room, replicated conditions prevailing, minus the replacement timber.

'Thank you for uncovering the weakness in my security measures, Lucille.'

RED DOCK

Time to have another talk with 'Apropos'. The bastard had double-crossed me by the way. He was supposed to deal with Anne and Conor, but he just drove off.

I'd an idea what he was up to, so I got online and typed in 'Nice work, Cornelius.'

No response.

'You're not coming through.'

Still nothing. Strange, he was definitely at home. I was along the road from his place. Maybe he was in the jacks. He wasn't. He was in a huff.

'Gratuitous and unnecessary treatment of helpless animals' came back.

I was right – the bastard was an animal lover. Why would anybody give a fuck about a couple of farm animals? Fuck me, the things you have to put up with from serial killers. I ignored him.

'Nothing gratuitous or unnecessary tonight.'

'Tonight?'

'Two down, two to go.'

'I think not.'

I think not? Jesus, don't tell me his conscience was getting to him. 'We have an agreement, Cornelius.'

'Ah, my remuneration.'

I knew it. He'd refused to sketch Anne because he was sticking his arm in. I let on I didn't understand. 'What remuneration?'

'My fee.'

'Your *fee?* Me keeping my mouth shut about you's your fee.'

'We have gone beyond that juncture. Thus far I have assisted you in your endeavours. Were I to find myself apprehended, the authorities would investigate those who stand to benefit from the deceased. You.'

He was up to something.

'Only one of two people, save my guest, whom you ignored, could possibly know my identity,' he typed. He'd removed the camera I'd fixed to his laptop. It didn't matter: text would be just as damning when the time came. 'And one of them, Greg Swags, is in custody. Which leaves you.'

Yeah, but there's no way you could know who I am.

'Therefore,' he typed on, 'since it is in both our interests to keep silent about the other, and because it is likely that you are acting for monetary gain, am I unreasonable in wishing to share in your good fortune?'

Bit of a money-grabber that Picasso. I wouldn't fancy standing at a bar with him – he'd let you buy all the drink.

'What have you got in mind?'

'Unless I am very much mistaken, you have in your

possession evidence which could be used to compromise Gemma Small's gentlemen friends, apropos their families, in return for payment?'

He was bound to have worked out that a blackmailing scam was on the go.

'Go on.'

'Since you are as yet unable to avail of what I surmise to be your "windfall" at the riding stables, I propose that you overcome the little matter of my advance fee by furnishing personal details and video recordings of two of Gemma's clients.'

'Why?'

'I can then apprise them of my understanding of their current vulnerability.'

The bastard wanted to blackmail them. Smart lad, that Picasso, even if he was a bit pompous. The 'windfall' remark wasn't important. He'd obviously been trying to make sense of what I was up to and had come up wrong. It didn't matter. If giving him a few punters got me what I wanted, fuck it, who cares?

I played along. 'I'll send you one now, and one when you've earned it.'

'One might prove risky. Two would reduce the possibility.'

'Explain.'

'I think not.'

Wonder what he had in mind?

'OK, two.'

'Appreciated. Naturally I shall require two who are of sufficient funds.'

'Done.'

'Following their receipt, I shall then await your instructions.'

I sent his laptop what he wanted so he could record it onto videotapes himself. It took a fair bit of time to transfer, but I could hardly deliver it by hand.

PICASSO

Having given the matter further consideration, I quickly came to the conclusion that my position was tenuous after all. Enhancing equipment might provide a better image but of whom? I would have no name, no address, merely film of an unknown man leaving the riding stables. Hardly proof of culpability with which to threaten him. Also, what if he did *not* attend the Donavans' funeral. His identity would continue to remain a mystery.

In short: I had decided to prolong our association. I would have more time to, as it were, flush him out. And the longer I was of use, the longer it would be before his evidence against me would be handed over to the authorities.

Furthermore, I had sensed an opportunity – one which I was determined to exploit.

Blackmail: the 'drop' – the appointed place to which the blackmail*ee* delivers payment – posed no obstacle. However, the 'pickup' – the point where the black-mail*er* takes possession – carried with it the risk of

apprehension, the police closing in and so forth. I therefore undertook its execution with care and diligence.

Personal security, as you will no doubt appreciate,
often resides in anonymity. Mine being precious to
me for reasons other than this foray into extortion, I
had to ensure that I did not become compromised. I
circumvented this by insisting on footage of Gemma
with not one but two of her clients, a Mr Agnew and
a Mr Webb, as it transpired. Each was worth in excess
of a half a million pounds. Ten per cent seemed a fair
amount to request, plus expenses.

I then availed myself of a battered green free-stand-
ing municipal waste bin, which I had found against a
hedge bordering a field on a narrow country road. In
my cellar I cut off the lower part of the back of the bin,
fitted hinges to it then screwed it back into its original
position, effectively creating a flap door. In the bottom of the inside I placed a metal box with a split,
self-closing lid (I had made this myself), attached to it
a long length of thick catgut then returned the finished
item to where I had found it. I removed enough of the
bottom of the hedge to allow the box to pass from
the bin through to the field and from there across the
grass to where I would be waiting to take possession
of its contents.

I then rang Mr Agnew to acquaint him with my
proposal.

'Mr Agnew?'

'Speaking.'

'Permit me to introduce myself. I am the man who

forwarded you a copy of your good self with a young woman in the Top Towers Hotel.'

'Just who do you think you are?'

Odd – I thought I had just informed him. 'May one ask if you have had an opportunity to view the merchandise on offer?'

'What?'

'I'm enquiring as to how you rated your performance.'

'Are you trying to be funny?'

'Merely interested in those with whom I conduct business.'

'I'll call the Guards.'

'How very kind. But, unlike yourself, I am not fond of handcuffs. Gemma seemed quite attached to them though. I see you enjoyed her in the traditional Christian praying position. And in the praying-to-Mecca position.'

'What the hell do you want?'

'To assure your peace of mind.'

'How much?'

'Shall we say £60,000?'

'Are you fucking mad?'

'How thoughtful of you to ask. Now, I do hope seven o'clock this evening does not inconvenience you. Deliver your donation, wrapped in a black bin liner, to the first roadside waste bin you come to past the Horse and Jockey public house going south on the Wexford road out of Dublin. Good morning.'

I then rang client number two.

'Am I addressing a Mr Webb?'

'Speaking.'

'Mr Webb, are you at liberty to converse on a matter of some delicacy?'

'Eh?'

'Is it safe for you to speak without the risk of being overheard?'

'It is. Who's this?'

'One who has your good name at heart. I feel it is my duty to apprise you on a matter which has come to my attention concerning a girl with whom you spent some time at the Top Towers Hotel.'

'I don't know what you're talking about.'

'I quite understand. Let me preface that which I am about to divulge by assuring you that I seek not to profit from this exchange. Suffice it to say that your liaison with the girl was secretly filmed.'

'*What?*'

'I'm afraid so.'

'Jesus Christ!'

'Quite.'

'What is it you want?'

'To inform you as to where the evidence can be retrieved.'

'In return for?'

'Not a thing.'

'I don't understand. You wouldn't be telling me this without wanting something.'

'I will leave the item for you taped to the inside of a waste bin.' I instructed him accordingly. 'Arrive this evening at eight o'clock sharp, and you will find it waiting for you.'

'Why are you doing this?'

'Call it my good deed for the day. Goodbye.'

Now for those of you who might be wondering why I had gone to these lengths, the explanation came in the form of Mr Agnew at the appointed hour. He put the package into the waste bin, its own weight then carried it down through the false floor to the box which I had constructed and the split lid sprang back, reinstating the base to its original position. He took a moment or two to furtively reconnoitre the surrounding area, perhaps in the expectation that I might put in an appearance, then drove away.

An hour later Mr Webb arrived and removed a videotape which I had taped behind the lid of the bin then departed unencumbered. Which told me that Mr Agnew had not involved the police. Had he, they would have assumed that Mr Webb was busying himself in the bin's interior to extract the cash and that he had perpetrated the incident.

They would have closed in. When they did not, I, as an extra precaution, went to the far side of the field, having waited for the cover of darkness and drew on the catgut, which pulled the box out of the bin and across to where I was happy to take possession of its contents.

I then rang Mr Webb.

'Mr Webb, I'm afraid I owe you an apology.'

'I don't see how.'

'Alas, the information I gave you was incorrect.'

'How?'

'Have you had the opportunity to view the tape?'

'Yeah.'

'Then I must inform you that a copy will be delivered to your wife.'

'*What?* But you said you didn't want any money.'

'An administrative error. Kindly place £60,000 in cash in the same waste bin tomorrow evening at seven sharp. Good night.'

I then rang Mr Agnew.

'Mr Agnew, I trust you are well.'

'Uh?'

'I neglected to leave you the master copy.'

He sounded suspicious. 'Eh?'

'Return to the same waste bin tomorrow evening at eight o'clock and you will find that it has been taped to the inside of the lid. You may take possession and conclude the transaction. Goodbye.'

The reverse now applied. If Mr Webb decided to alert the authorities, they would then have been in a position to observe Mr Agnew's eight o'clock appearance. He would have been seen as the perpetrator. You will be delighted to hear that Mr Webb deposited the cash into the bin, Mr Agnew later retrieved his so-called 'master' copy and I took into my bosom the second £60,000. I'd received £120,000. I was not displeased.

RED DOCK

Corn doesn't take any chances. He got those two punters of Gemma's to pay him by playing one off against the other in case the law turned up. Crafty bastard. I might use that trick myself sometime. I'd tailed him to see how he'd do it. He was in the vicinity, they made the drops then he disappeared into a field before heading off. Alternative uses for waste bins. Anyway, his *fee* had been well paid – that was the main thing. Time to make him work for it.

I got on to his laptop and told him to get his scalpels sharpened.

Then I went to visit my family – what was left of it. I was gonna get Corn to deal with Conor as well as Anne, but I was wise to the bastard: he'd only do one then demand a couple more of Gemma's punters before doing the other. I wanted it over with, so I decided to do Conor myself.

The same method of thinking applied. This would later seem like Lucille's handiwork.

I parked along the road and cut up through the

fields to Conor's place. I didn't tell him his brother was coming home to see him or anything; wanted it to be a surprise. Family members are always surprising one another, or so I'm told. I only know about families from what I'm told, and from what I'm told, I'm glad I only know what I'm told.

Not that Conor would see it like that. After I'd finished with him, he wouldn't be seeing anything. I'd brought him a little goodbye present: formaldehyde and potassium permanganate.

He goes around checking his stock, y'see, before calling it a night. He was turning the key in the tack room when I commenced my homecoming.

'Well, brother,' I said, 'how's it going?' The 'brother' bit didn't register. He thought I was using it in the colloquial sense. Startled the shit out of him though, me stepping out from behind his horsebox, but he didn't say as much; just a quick check of the old composure, then a 'Who are you?' Marvellous, isn't it – all these years and not even as much as a hug.

'Inside.' This startler worked better: it was made of iron and fired bullets. Though, as with Skeffington, I'd no intentions of shooting him either. But again, he didn't know that. Information technology, y'see – you can't beat it. He hesitated though, looked me up and down. I doubt he was considering having a go – there was twenty feet between us. He'd never've made it. Besides, maybe I'd just called to warn him about something not shoot him. Bullshit of course. But people's minds start calculating all sorts of possibilities in a situation like

190

this, all to persuade themselves that the trigger won't get pulled if they cooperate. I'd say Conor was doing much the same. He'd probably no wads of cash lying around, no one was after him for anything illegal, he'd nothing to be blackmailed with. A nice clean life. He probably thought I'd got the wrong guy. If he'd known what I had in my head, that tack room was the last place he'd have gone into.

'So how's life treating you, Conor?'

'Who are you?'

'Red Dock. I introduced myself to you twenty years ago. Don't tell me you forgot. And surely the word "brother" must've given you a clue.'

'What brother? I have no brother.'

'Ah, I see, so you indulged yourself in a bit of selective memory. Common enough in this game. It's amazing what people's consciences'll let them forget.'

'Look, I don't know who you are or what this is about, but I have no brother and I don't know you.'

'You didn't know me the last time I was up here. Oddly enough, watching you that day gave me the idea of how to pull this off. I wasn't relative to you then either, so you wouldn't remember. You were lunging a horse. I was impressed by the way you had it rearing and boxing. A foot closer and it would've hit you a dig in the mouth. One punch'd've done it. It would've trotted off – no hoofprints taken, no charges brought. Most people wouldn't look at it like that of course. I seem to be always on the lookout for ways to make the law see things the way I want them to, though it took me years to figure out how to get a horse to hit someone a dig in the mouth. My sister, as it happens. Sorry, mustn't forget *you* in this – "our" sister.'

Good actor, my brother. 'Our' sister? was popping out of him like he was genuinely puzzled by it. But I was definitely getting through to him. There's nothing like a good murder picture when it comes to shocking an audience. And of course he was glaring at me like I was the bad guy. No doubt he was casting himself as the aggrieved hero. 'You killed Edna, you dirty rat' was written all over his face. No, it wasn't. He wasn't that quick, but it was on the way. The law'd spent a couple of days taping off the scene, getting the coroner to do his Picasso impersonation. They'd dig two of those holes I was telling you about earlier and fuck the pair of them in. Conor didn't even know they'd been the victims of a boxing horse and a load of old bull. Mixing my metaphors here. Is 'boxing horse' a metaphor? Don't know. Who cares about crap like that? Conor was looking like he wished one would prance in and lay one on me. I don't think he wanted me for a brother. Homecomings can be so disappointing.

He was a good actor all right. He nearly had me convinced he didn't know what I was talking about. And there was me intending to tell him all about what I'd been up to: Doctor Skeffington, for instance, but I knew I'd be wasting my breath. He should've gone to RADA. By my calculations, he'd've been fourteen when me and Sean were born. Old enough to know what the bump in our mother's stomach meant. He'd've hit me with 'I thought she'd miscarried' or some shit like that. I'd had it in mind to tell him about Lucille and who she thought she was and about her old man, who was part of a police force who'd been trained to notice their own kids being taken away but not thousands of other kids – kids like me and Sean. I'd definitely intended to tell him about Sean; how he'd died. But it sickened me to see him standing there with a pile of 'I didn't knows' on his tongue. A woman has kids who disappear and it's a topic of whispers in the family. He knew all right. I wasn't going to let him demean Sean's memory by denying he knew. Fuck it, I could go on like this forever. Whatever he'd said, I wasn't believing it. If he'd wanted to find us, he could have. He didn't, so fuck him. The Donavans walked away from us. We didn't even exist to them. Not that Sean ever believed that.

Sean used to say that it would all turn out to be some big mistake; maybe we'd got lost and Mammy hadn't been able to find us, and she was crying for us. Well, I made Sean a promise, and I was just keeping that promise, and I'd learnt from those who brought me up that you could get away with a whole manner of things simply by making the law view you in a certain light. And that's what I was doing.

If I'd said to Conor stuff like: the law'd do me for putting Lucille through an abusive orphanage system, but that same law had no notion of doing the hundreds of so-called innocent clergy who stood by and watched thousands of kids being handed in, knowing their peers would abuse them, he'd have looked at me as if I was talking a foreign language. The sort of stuff people who hadn't been through it tell you should be forgotten.

I'm rambling here. Didn't mean to do that. Facing him after all this time had sort of got the old nerves jumping.

'Bye, bro.'

I locked the door on my way out.

Now this tack room of my brother's had no windows in it, but it did have a small ventilation hole in the door. And the method I'd come up with for him had to do with a virus called strangles. It can live on tack. You can pick it up on your hand and pass it on to a horse, and that'll be the end of it. A growth swells in its windpipe and it dies gasping for breath – no cheese wire or ropes required – unless it gets a dose of modern antibiotics, though that doesn't work in all cases.

While Conor had been out checking his stock, I'd found an ice-cream container in the tack room and nailed it to the inside of the door. And now it was time to pour the formaldehyde in through the hole into the container. Then came the potassium permanganate. I'd brought my own in case he was out. But I'd seen his supply on the shelf and used it. Better for the law to think his had been used. It wouldn't point to an outsider. It would point to Lucille.

Potassium permanganate looks like coal particles. Mixed with formaldehyde, it forms what's called formalin. It's a gas. Though Conor didn't think so. He wasn't laughing anyway. Mind you, he was the one breathing it in. Formalin gas kills strangles. And anything else. That's why it's best to do it from the outside. Go in there and you won't come out. It acts in seconds. White smoke everywhere and bonk! down you go.

Now I don't know if you've ever heard a man being gassed. But it's a noisy business. I suppose you'd have to imagine some cunt locking you in a room then tossing in a canister. Going mad to get out pretty much describes how people react to it. You've never heard the like of it in your life. Grabbing and tearing at that ice-cream container he was, trying to get it off. Which he did. Well, ice-cream containers aren't that hard to remove. I think he was exploring the possibility of bunging his mouth in the hole for a breath of nice country air. Then again, they say the night air's not good for you. I felt fine though. Of course, while tearing the container off, he had to come into closer contact with it, which rather defeats the object. He was breathing it in all the more. Once the formaldehyde and that other stuff make contact, as the saying goes: 'What I have mixed together let no man put asunder.' Didn't do much for his nails, I can tell you that. Some of the gas escaped through the hole, as gas will, but there was plenty left for him.

Interesting what good screamers men make at times like this. I'd never heard no woman scream like that. Still, it didn't last. It turned into a croak before very long. The old 'aaghhhh … aaghhh … aagh' becoming an 'aa … a …' until he hadn't an 'a' to his name. With no window, it had nowhere to go but him. It's a question of physics, y'see. You have to be up on that stuff to be able to pull a stroke like this.

I didn't wait much after Conor'd stopped. No point. I'd other things to do. I wiped my prints off the door handle and bolt and withdrew the bolt, so it was almost open but not quite. Part of that method thinking I mentioned.

I didn't go out and celebrate. This wasn't about victory. Just clearing up some outstanding business.

All I had to do now was go back to my car, get my laptop out and contact Cornelius.

'Anne Donavan is awaiting your immediate attention,' I typed. 'She'll make a good model for you.'

PICASSO

It had occurred to me that my position, still tenuous, would fortify were I to withdraw my services in their entirety. Amy and Edna Donavan's deaths were not attributable to me. Were their niece, Anne, however, discovered bearing my *signature* that perception would alter. I therefore ignored instructions to proceed to the riding stables post haste. In short, with reference to earlier conjecture, I was now convinced that my visiting Anne Donavan would be the knell of my usefulness, not my arrest, resulting in my experiencing some prearranged fatal mishap, courtesy of my blackmailer, whereupon the police would deduce that I, and I alone, had been responsible for all three deaths chez Donavan, leaving him to benefit unhindered and beyond apprehension. I confess that I could not elucidate upon this hypothesis, except to propound that it was abundantly clear that my welfare would be low on his agenda. Such was my reading.

I ignored the communication, hoping to prolong our association further, until I had taken ameliorative steps to safeguard my personal safety. Alas …

RED DOCK

Well, well, well. So Picasso was double-crossing me again. I dunno, y'give a man two names to blackmail and what appreciation do you get? I mean if a man can't rely on his own personal killer, who can he rely on? Sure now. Life's full of little disappointments.

'"Apropos", what the fuck's the crack?' I typed him.

Nothing. He never answered. The cunt was probably still in his scratcher. Anybody'd think he was working late. Not for me he wasn't. 'This is not satisfactory,' I hit him with. 'Apro-fucking-pos our gentleman's agreement.'

That's the trouble with crime these days: no fucker's reliable.

'OK, Corn, this is the way it is. I tried to be reasonable, and you won't let me. So your mother will get a copy of your activities.'

'Done.'

'Ah, that's better.'

I told him what I wanted him to do then waited to make sure he did it.

PICASSO

Pressure had been exerted on me which I had not anticipated. I was compelled to visit the riding stables and liaise with Anne Donavan.

I was surprised to see that while she was pretty, in her own country-girl way, ideal for a bringing-in-the-hay portrait, she bore no resemblance whatsoever to her daughter. Still, she did have rather fine skin …

I began with a conventional expression of 'Good evening', which elicited a guarded 'Hello'. The late hour, a stranger at the door, the remote location, the aura of recent events, her aunts' demise, for whom her slightly puffed eyes suggested that she had been crying, their funeral, due the following day, and so forth were no doubt unsettling to her.

'May I come in?'

'Who are you?'

'An associate of your daughter's.'

'My daughter's? I have no daughter.'

'Quite. However, I am privy to information to the contrary: Frances Anne Donavan, also known as Lucille Kells.'

'What are you talking about?'

'I too feel the matter requires elucidation.'

My chloroform spray rendered her incapacitated. I bound her hands behind her back and laid her out in the first double-bedded room that presented itself – her father's, as I was later to discover – and waited while she regained consciousness.

'You have a relative who walks with a limp?'

'No. Look, please tell me what this is all about. Who *are* you? Why are you doing this to me? Why?'

Fear inspires many questions.

'In the event of your father's death, who, save yourself, stands to inherit?'

'What?'

'Please answer.'

'No one. Cousins … I don't know.'

'No one specifically?'

'No. It would be shared out, I suppose. Why? Why are you asking me this?'

'Lucille's Kells' father – he walks with a limp?'

'I don't even know who Lucille's father is.'

'You had several lovers?'

'"Several lovers"?'

I produced Lucille's birth certificate. 'You still deny this?'

'I've never seen it before. Or Lucille, up until recently.'

The conundrum at hand had now been rendered fathomable by further reflection. And although Anne Donavan was refusing to put construction to the truth, it was the case that mothers had been known to deny having given their children into care, even when official documents proved the contrary. Perhaps she was lying to protect the father. Perhaps he was behind this, manipulating events which would allow his daughter to claim the family fortune. He could then re-enter Lucille's life and share in her inheritance. Whatever Anne Donavan's reasoning, she would reveal to me the truth surrounding the affair. I would then know exactly why I had been blackmailed into killing Lucille's family.

RED DOCK

I have to report that me old mate Picasso went to see Anne and left her in need of a few stitches.

I waited for an hour or so after he'd gone then took a drive up to the main house and went inside. Anne was in Conor's bedroom, relaxing against the pillows. Not the sort of thing you should look at on a full stomach. You'd throw up. I'd seen corpses before but, fuck me, never the way Picasso left them.

Her hair was draping down around the edges of what his gallery suggested was a carved flower. Her legs were spread wide. Oddly enough they were still attached to her. Maybe he forgot his saw. She was a bad colour too, pale as the sheets – pale and *red* as the sheets. Her arms were detached though, spread out from her crotch to make her look like she'd four legs. She wouldn't be showing any more mares, that was for sure.

I wasn't interested in trying to figure out why he'd cut her the way he had. I had what I wanted and that was that.

I'd had enough of fucking around with the Donavans.

It was over. Besides, this wasn't even my home. It held fuck all for me. It hadn't even been built when Sean and I were born. The cottage was. That's where I'd watched Picasso coming and going from. We'd been born there. Skeffington had more or less confirmed it.

Nice little cottage. Modernised now, but it still held its charm. I began in the kitchen, checking, as I'd checked before for something to do with my past. I didn't expect to find anything this time either. And I wasn't disappointed.

But then something hit me. It was the eyes that did it. Y'know how the eyes in some pictures follow you around the room? Well, that's what the Sacred Heart was doing. I thought of something a nun had said to me when I was a kid. She was one of the good ones.

'Robert,' she said. 'Folk'll take down every picture in the house except a Sacred Heart.' Which didn't make any sense to me at first, until she went on. 'They admire family photos and take them down, pass them around at gatherings and so on.' She'd been referring to the twenties and thirties when photos were a big thing; when people paid a lot of attention, wanted to know what had become of such and such who'd fucked off to America and years later had sent home a picture of what he looked like now, which his folks then showed to people who'd known him when he was young. But a Sacred Heart's a Sacred Heart, so nobody had any reason to take one down for a closer look.

I took down Edna's and there taped to the back was

a letter, dated the night I was born, from the old girl herself, Teresa Donavan. My darling fucking mother.

Dear Conor, Edna and Amy,

My darling children, I never wanted to go away and leave you, but I had to go. Some day you'll understand the reason why. I didn't want you coming back to an empty house wondering what had become of me, so I'm leaving this note to say that everything will be clear when I see you again.

Your ever-loving mother

It was too vague. But it more or less fitted in: she'd got herself into trouble and was going off to dump me and Sean in the orphanage because bringing up a couple of illegitimate kids'd bring shame on the family. As I say, the nature of illegitimacy in Ireland ruled out ever discovering the truth behind it. That's why people like me exist. Still, that's the way it goes. No good complaining. You have to make the best of the opportunities life has given you. The Donavans got rid of me and Sean; I got rid of them. 'An eye for an eye', as the guy in the picture hiding the note'd once said. I'm very religious when it comes to certain things the Church teaches us.

Speaking about the Church, I forgot to tell you exactly where I knew Picasso from. Me and him had shared a well once. It was actually a dried-up well. They used to lower you down in a bucket then close the top off.

Punishment stuff. I got mine for creeping out of bed one night to see how Sean was doing. Corn got his for asking too many questions – one.

A government minister visited the place one day and Corn went up to him.

'Might I have a word?' he asked. 'Are you in a position to prevent them from treating us like this?' I'll never forget it. Only Corn could've put it like that. We all started giggling.

The minister didn't though. He looked at his chauffeur and said, 'Get me to fuck out of this place.' His exact words for all to hear and from a minister too. Tut tut.

The Brothers weren't mad about it either. Corn had been there only a few weeks, y'see. He hadn't been educated to their ways yet.

You always knew when someone important was coming to see them. Usually it was an orphanage inspector who came. He'd run a check on how we were being treated, and that'd be him for another year. He'd just drive off in his black Austin with running boards on the sides and let on he'd suffered some sort of perception blackout, that he hadn't seen what he'd seen.

Anyway, Corn worked on the farm feeding the pigs. If the Brothers liked you, they'd give you a cushy job. And they liked Corn. Which meant he got plenty to eat. The meals there were bread and dripping for breakfast, a kind of porridge at midday, cabbage and the water from the cabbage and spuds for dinner, and an egg every Easter. But if you worked with the pigs, you got what they got. You made yourself Head Pig. The best job of course was going around the canteen unstitching mice from the gunge they used to tape onto skirting boards. You could usually grab a handful of something.

Now because this diet hardly led to what you'd call healthy teeth and bones, it meant that we were all skinny little bastards, stunted and full of boils. Our necks used to be covered in them.

So when a big shot was calling, they'd get you up, cover you with a white dust to hide the boils – some of those big shots must've let themselves believe they'd walked into a bakery – and give you new sheets, pillow-cases, new plates and cups, good silverware and decent clothes. It would all disappear and we'd be back into our sack clothes once he was out the door. But Corn had disappeared before this minister'd showed up.

He'd been feeding the pigs in his normal gear and when he came back and the minister saw the difference between him and us, he knew that Corn's gear was the norm, and the Brothers knew he knew it. But Corn took this as a good opportunity to ask his question. It's hard to believe that someone with enough brains to outwit the law was once so naïve.

He got slaughtered for it. The door to the whip room opened and they put his head up against a Brother's crotch and laid into him naked in front of the rest of us. I think the Brothers felt he'd let them down. Corn lost his pig job after that. We had to carry him to the infirmary and lay him out. I knew he was in for what they called the 'head staggers' after that.

They had a night watchman, y'see, who used to go around the dorms with this birch, some old branch he'd broken off a tree. He'd lay into whoever took his fancy. Or whoever had embarrassed his bosses. The beds were laid with their foots at the windows and their heads at the centre aisle. Everybody had to sleep in the same direction: you had to lie on your left side with your back to the door. The watchman used to come in from behind you, and you weren't allowed to look round, so you never knew he was going to pick on you until you felt the birch. A lot of kids were afraid to go back to sleep again. You were always jumping at the slightest noise, steeling yourself. Corn got that night in, night out, for fuck knows how long. That and the constant digs in the head was how they'd give you the staggers. He was one of the lucky ones – he never went deaf over it. Oh, and the bat and ball. A Brother'd put him against a wall and fire hurling balls at his head. All this stuff went on for months, years sometimes, till they had you going around banging your head against the wall. Some banged their heads that much they lost eyes, smashed bones, all that. It was their way of driving you insane. Then they'd send you off to the nuthouse.

It's amazing how many people are surprised to learn that Brothers only joined up for a job for life. Bit like joining the army. No sense of vocation or fuck all like that. Funnily enough, I never saw Corn banging his head against the wall. That surprised me. Anyway, they'd stick you in the well as well. That's where I got to know him better. His voice, in particular, I should say. It was too dark to see his face.

I think I remember him telling me his parents were in a bad car crash, and Corn ended up in with me for a couple of years while they were getting better. Corn wasn't a long-termer. A lot of kids spent time in those homes because their parents had fallen on hard times for a while and had no one else to turn to for help. Some of them even came from families who could've looked after them but wouldn't – they'd gone to America or whatever – and left them in what they'd thought were good hands, even paid for them to be looked after. Corn's parents probably thought he was having a great time. Once they were better of course they came and got him.

Funny how things work out.

Though funny isn't a word that came to mind when I rehung that Sacred Heart. I wasn't alone in that cottage.

'Well, this is a surprise.'

'What?'

I didn't even see it coming. It was Corn. Complete with spray. He let me have it.

PICASSO

Having questioned Anne Donavan apropos Lucille Kells/Frances Anne Donavan, I had watched the entrance to the stables from a hedge behind the cottage. A man approached. He was walking with a limp. In the light of the kitchen, where he discovered a letter behind a Sacred Heart picture, I found myself recalling an acquaintance from my youth. I have touched on this on a prior occasion and, although I saw no reason to expand at that time, I feel that I should do so now.

I once had the misfortune to experience the inhospitality of a home for boys. An 'industrial school' to give it its designated title. I lay one particular night on a bed recovering from a flogging. And that very morning a boy, known to me as Sean Dock, had found himself in the enviable position of being unable to consume his breakfast of bread and dripping. Sean had explained that he was unwell to the Brother in charge, who then administered what he, and others of that institution, referred to as 'a good kicking'. Or, in the Brother's case, a good kick*ing*. He has the most irritating habit of emphasising his 'G's. Even now it is impossible to hear anyone of that inclination without thinking of that Brother.

Earlier that morning we were awoken, as was the practice, to the command: 'Up, up, sailors in line.'

Sailors – those who had wet their beds – were required to form a line. As an added disincentive, boys who had brothers were forced to undergo beatings at their hands. Implements were furnished for this purpose, and Sean Dock, a nightly offender, was punished each dawn by his twin, Red. Sean, naked, would bend over, and Red would have to administer the strap.

Red would register his objections, which led to he himself being strapped. This would cease only when he agreed to comply. They would beat him until he agreed to beat his brother. Sean, however, was a sickly boy, and the effect of this rendered him incapable of eating. The nerves in his tummy, I suppose, prevented comfortable digestion. In that sense, Red had unwillingly induced this nausea, its result having invited 'a good kicking'. The Brother responsible then dragged the unconscious boy to the infirmary.

That night I found myself waking to a conversation. Red was by Sean's bed. Both were whispering.

'Robert,' Sean was saying, 'how do you prove you're being good?'

Robert – Red was a nickname because of his hair colouring – did not have an answer. I myself would have been at a loss to provide one. Regardless of conduct, all were treated as offenders, constantly abused into believing that we had been abandoned by our families, who did not want us, because we were no good and never would be. Why this conviction was instilled, that all that had befallen us at the hands of the clergy was our families' doing, in Red's case, for sixteen years – from infancy to the time of his release – was never explained.

Sean then referred to their family.

'You'll tell them about me, Robert, won't you?'

'Sean, you can tell them yourself. You'll get better.'

Sean seemed of a different opinion. 'Promise me you'll tell them about me, Robert.'

'Sean, for fuck's sake quit talking like that.'

'Promise.'

'Sean, you'll get better. You'll be going home.'

'Promise you'll take me home and bury me.'

Red simply could not deal with the situation. Sean knew he was dying and the only thing that would console him was the promise. And Red made it.

'I promise,' he said, 'I promise.'

The door opened and Red's transgressions were discovered. He had crept out of bed and gone to his twin. I heard what happened to him moments later, as did Sean. I did not need to witness his punishment, having had some experience of it myself, to attest to its savagery.

It was their practice to spread malefactors naked on the bottom of a staircase and administer a section of tyre from a pram wheel until the welts satisfied their appetites.

The following morning I was lowered into a well,

where I found Red. We spent some forty-eight hours or so huddled together.

In Ireland, besides those found in churchyards, there are three kinds of cemeteries. One, for children born dead: not having been baptised, the original mark of Adam still on their souls, they cannot lie in consecrated ground. Two, the cemetery of the institution: for the religious. Three, an adjoining plot: for boys who have died while in care.

Red absconded and was discovered weeping over Sean's grave, in which four other boys had also been buried. 'They even got the date wrong,' he said. 'Sean died on the fourteenth. They put the fifteenth.'

He had seen Sean alive after midnight and so was aware of the error. Had they monitored the boy's condition, they too would have known.

Thereafter, Red, to the religious, remained bright and cocky, a demeanour he maintained, refusing to show the effects of his twin's death. In private, such privacy as could be obtained within those confines, he became increasingly insular and motivated. He had an infinite number of ideas – get-rich schemes by the mountainload. Where he conjured them from, and to what end, only he knew; he would have made a formidable scholar, an addition to any society. He had also deduced the ways in which the clergy kept their records. One theory was that, in the case of children who had known no other upbringing than the system, by using the first two letters of an inmate's name – he referred to himself as an inmate – one could ascertain the beginning of one's birth name, and by applying the same logic to the last letters one's place of birth. In short, the letters D-O-C-K now suggested to me that Red's real name began with 'DO', for Donavan, ending in 'CK', for Clonkeelin, Kildare. Red was a Donavan. Used as a method of decoding, the name Kells did not enter its parameters. Lucille was not a Donavan, Red was.

In light of the unexplained coincidence of having found him in the cottage on the night of Anne's death, I had decided to bring him back to my rooms for questioning. And now, with Lucille in the next room, I began.

RED DOCK

'Corn, me old mate, how's it going? What the fuck's that rustling noise?'

'A little interrogation technique of my own design. The rat in the corner is enjoying a piece of raw meat. His colleagues are inside the crate gnawing their way through.'

'How long will it take them?'

'Usually several days.'

'They'll be famished by then.'

'They are hoping you fail to answer my questions truthfully.'

'How many are there?'

'Three dozen.'

'Questions?'

'Rats.'

'What if you're called out?'

'I have furnished a replacement timber, hammer and nails to allow you to shore off the crate temporarily thus prolonging their escape. You could of course always hit them with the hammer.'

'What if you're held up?'

'I would inform those holding me up where to find you. One week later.'

'They'll be finding us both, Corn. By tomorrow, I'd say.' I had his attention. 'C'mere a minute, Corn.' I didn't want Lucille hearing what I had to say. 'Why don't we go down to your art gallery and have a little talk?'

'I think not.'

'Corn, I'm not likely to be making a run for it with those dogs on the end of my bollocks. Besides, you know what I've been up to. Even if I got out of here, I couldn't turn you in, any more than you could me. So what's there to be lost? More importantly, what's there to be gained? By you.'

Greed, y'see. He was always a greedy bastard, even when we were emailing each other he was always after as good a deal as he could get.

'You have another of your get-rich plans in mind?'

'When they were dishing out plans, they must've mistaken me for an architect – and given me a whole drawerful.'

He thought about it long enough to see that he'd nothing to lose, then opened the door.

'Good man. C'mon.' And down we went.

'I've admired your paintings. That *Duet* has something going for it.'

'Thank you.'

'I'm glad you don't like painting men. I wouldn't fancy being in one of them. I know all about the flowers.

215

I read about it in your journal.' Y'shoulda seen the one called *January*. The girl in it had a face like a shovel – a crooked chin and a twisted nose. Meet her on a dark night and you'd shit yourself.

'What do you call them? The "Calendar Collection"?'

'Actually, no, though that is a possibility.'

'It lacks something.'

'Oh?'

'Enigma.'

'Explain.'

Packing crates were in the centre of the room.

'You're sending them away?'

'To international galleries. Artists do like to display their work.'

'Most of them don't exhibit anonymously. You should give them more to ponder over. As it is, they'll wonder why you didn't complete the collection by including a *December*.'

'An omission to be rectified this evening.'

'Bad move. Let *Duet* take its place. Let them wonder why you did that. Complete it and *Duet* will look out of place. It won't fit in. Send it as it is, and they'll have more to talk about.'

It seemed to amuse him. 'You know, Red, you might just have hit on something there.'

'So you can forget about *December*.'

'What exactly are you leading up to, Red?'

'Business. Lucille thinks Anne Donavan's her old dear.'

'She is not.'

'How do you know?'

'I questioned her most persuasively. You did insist that I visit her. She endured my interrogation unnecessarily, when a simple confirmation of that which Lucille's birth certificate had already proven to me would have granted her an easier passing. Lucille may think she is her mother. I myself am convinced that she is not.'

'Yeah, well, it's what Lucille *thinks* that counts.'

'A plot which you constructed?'

'Presentation, Corn. If there's one thing I learnt from those who put us in that well, it was that. I've seen to it the law'll see Lucille as being behind this. When she's convicted, I claim what's mine and Sean rests easy. That's all I want. I've nothing personal against Lucille. Only ...'

'Yes?'

'They'll be grabbing you as well.'

'I see.'

'Unless we do a deal.'

It was my only way out of there. 'The computer I used to email you shows you at the Top Towers Hotel. I get out of here, the law don't find it with your name on it. You keep me here, they do. That's the deal.' I was tempting him. He knew as well as I did that if he let me go we could never squeal on each other without landing both of us in it. I'd have nothing to fear from him, and, more importantly, from his end, he'd have nothing to fear from me. 'And I'll throw in another dozen of Gemma's punters for you to practise your waste-bin routine on.'

'A dozen?'

Think how many scalpels that'd buy. 'But there's one proviso – Lucille has to be released.'

'Impossible.'

'Corn, all she can give the law is a description of a tall blonde guy with a cellar that could be anywhere in the thirty-two counties. OK, there's a risk. But there's always a risk. Steer clear of women's prisons and she won't be able to ID you from behind a forty-foot wall and tip them off. Hang on to me and that risk becomes a sure thing: you'll be spending the rest of your natural in a room not much different from the one you had me in. Decision time, Corn.'

I had him. In his position, I'd've run with it. And so would he. What did he have to lose for fuck's sake?

And the beauty of it was: Greg Swags'd be released. Corn leaving his mark on Anne'd see to that. Winters'd still try to hold Greg of course. No doubt he'd come up with some crap like Corn and Greg were partners. But partners wouldn't fight it out in a hotel room, leaving one unconscious to identify the other. It'd never stand up. He'd let him go all right.

'The longer you wait, Corn, the more chance they have of finding that laptop. And only I know where it is.'

'You are very persuasive, Red.'

'I just see the angles, Corn.'

'Tell me, did you manage to fulfil your ambition and become a millionaire?'

'I'm a success story, Corn. And chew on this: do you

think I'd be handing you a deal if I thought it wasn't straight up? Because if it isn't, I won't be at liberty long enough to bring Sean home. And that's all I care about. No way would I jeopardise that. Done?'

'Done. But tell me, how have you arranged for Lucille to be apprehended?'

'Give her a whiff of that spray of yours and you'll find out. C'mon.'

ELEVEN MONTHS LATER

RED DOCK

Here was the prosecutor – Thomas Frederick Dunne, big-timer in the brief profession, big dorsal-fin snout, avoids floating on his back at the beach in case he starts a panic – 'Detective Sergeant Winters, the morning you were called to investigate the deaths of Amy and Edna Donavan, you initially considered deaths by misadventure I believe.' Big smirk. 'Why was that?'

'Because farm animals sometimes cause fatal accidents!'

Oops. Touchy. Notice the dash with the dot on the bottom of Chilly's response. That means Chilly's pissed off. What the smirk was really saying was, 'Lucille Kells must be very clever if she can fool a hardened cop like you into believing death by misadventure with bodies lying all over the place.' Tom Fred loves getting his neb in the papers with his courtroom antics – and playing to seven men and five women – three fuckable and two old dears – who made up the jury.

'It had been raining heavily the morning their bodies were discovered – any physical evidence which might have suggested foul play had been washed away. I spoke to Conor Donavan, asked him about the bolt in the bull's enclosure; had the wasps' nest been a problem before then; what would have brought Edna Donavan out into the field in the early hours of the morning? He had no answers. Things happen. He saw nothing more to it than that. Short of anything else to go on at that time, except the jarring coincidence of two people dying the same night, misadventure was a possibility!'

Bit of a mouthful there, Chill. Wanted everyone to know he knew a thing or two when it came to doing his Detective Bloggs bit — not to mention getting that 'jarring coincidence' line in so people wouldn't think he didn't see it.

'The Donavans' vet was called to examine a foal I believe.'

'Yes.'

'And what was his diagnosis?'

'Your Honour'—that was Brady, Lucille's man – the only thing big time about him is the grandfather clock covering the damp patch in his hall—'if the prosecution wishes to enter the professional findings of the vet, why doesn't he call him?'

'Your Honour, vets have been known to corroborate evidence given to police officers, in my experience. I have no objection to Mr Brady calling a vet, should he feel the need of one.'

'Yes, sit down, Mr Brady.' That was the judge – face like a chimp, avoids walking past pet shops in case they drag him in and stick him in the window.

'The vet said it was blind in one eye, its lungs hadn't formed, its coat was slack, its left foreleg was crooked, it couldn't get to its feet to suckle and eight hours or so had passed since birth, so it hadn't consumed the antibodies only present in the mare's milk for the first six hours, which foals need against infection.'

'What was the cause of the foal's condition?'

'It had been born six weeks prematurely.'

'His prognosis?'

Don't back it to win the Derby.

'He suggested putting it out of its misery. Conor Donavan agreed and asked him to carry out a post-mortem.'

'Is that standard procedure in the death of a foal?'

'The vet wanted to determine whether the mare had foaled early because of an infection. If so, it would have to be identified and treated before she was later served to prevent it being passed on to the stallion.'

'And the results of the post-mortem?'

'Traces of follicle-inducing stimulants were found in the foal's system.'

'And what is their relevance?'

'The mare had been fed them deliberately to bring her into labour.'

'Why would the Donavans do such a thing?'

'They didn't.'

Wonder who did.

Tom Fred knew.

'Lucille Kells, Detective Sergeant, when she was found unconscious in her holiday home, as part of your house-to-house inquiry'—me and Corn dropped her off—'what was found beside her?'

'Farming books.'

We dropped those off as well.

Tom Fred took them over to Chilly. 'Are these the books?'

'Yes.'

'Each has several pages folded. They were like that when you found them?'

'Yes.'

'What do they describe?'

'How mares and bulls have been known to cause fatal accidents and—'

Boring details establishing how big Ed and Amy came by the info first-hand.

'What else do they describe?'

'How to eradicate strangles.'

Boring details establishing Conor got eradicated the same way.

'What was found beside these books?'

'Lucille's birth certificate and a laptop.'

We dropped those off as well.

'What was recorded on the laptop?'

'Emails to Picasso.'

Boring details proving Corn was blackmailed into killing the Donavans.

'In Edna, Amy and Conor Donavan's case, was he instructed to use the same methods described in the farming books?'

'Yes.'

Stacks more stuff followed. Tom Fred should put me on his Christmas-card list. I'd given him enough evidence to choke *Jaws*. Any more and he'd've never got it in the fucking door.

Brady had a go.

'Detective Sergeant Winters, did Lucille explain *how* she came to be so easily found unconscious in her holiday home?'

'She has no knowledge of how she got there.'

We didn't tell her we'd be dropping her off unconscious.

'When she regained consciousness, what was her first concern?'

'She kept asking, "Is my mother all right? Please tell me my mother is all right."' (Her mother's fine, as far as I know. Mind you, I haven't seen her in twenty years. That reminds me, I told her I'd get back to her. Hope she's not still sitting in Whites' farmhouse waiting on my call.) 'When I told her that Anne Donavan had been murdered, she became even more hysterical. She was covered in bite marks. When I asked what had happened "Picasso's rats" was all that I could get out of her. Questioning had to wait until she'd been taken to the station and a doctor brought in.'

'Were you troubled at any time that the amount of evidence against Lucille was found so conveniently?'

'Really, Your Honour, perhaps Mr Brady would like to ask the accused if she too was troubled that the amount of evidence against her was found so conveniently?'

'Yes, I was troubled.'

'Why?'

'Because every question I put to Lucille had been answered "I don't know". A girl who'd pull a stroke like this would have all kinds of get-outs. But she hadn't one. A clever criminal on the one hand, a fool on the other. No poison had been used, no guns, no sticks or bats, no running people over, no pushing in front of trains or from high windows, no kickings, no drug overdoses. Three of the Donavans had been killed in ways I had never come across. There was a mind at work here. Yet how did that mind allow itself to get caught so easily?'

I think Chill had a soft spot for Lucille. A touch of compassion there in the way he said that. Maybe fathers who've had their daughters kidnapped and who find themselves charging them for murder twenty years later feel sorry for them automatically even though they don't know they're their daughters. That's just my theory. I doubt anyone's done a study. Maybe they tried but couldn't find any long-lost kidnapped daughters to question.

Next up came the shrinks, to explain how Lucille appeared to be unaware of the crimes she'd committed. One acting for her barrister, the other for the state. One for, one against.

The former said she had no memory of them because, in his view, she hadn't committed them. The latter said he reckoned she had a split personality. She had a good side – it came through when she was with people who'd been kind to her – and a bad – evil and cunning, which came through when she was with people who'd maltreated her.

Tom Fred brought in witnesses from the orphanage. They'd been seated outside and didn't know what the shrinks had said. A Sister Angeline said she was very fond of Lucille, that she was kind and compassionate. But when they called a Sister Dominic, and she said Lucille was anything but, everyone in the courtroom knew that she had maltreated her.

Here's what a reporter covering the trial wrote. (I got all this from the media by the way – I could hardly turn up in court and have Chilly thinking, 'Here, that's Red Dock. Wonder what he's doing here.') 'Sister Dominic wasn't aware as to why the hushed courtroom was looking at her accusingly. But the point had been substantiated. Lucille had an evil and cunning side.'

Lucille's turn.

'Lucille, while you were *deceiving* your mother, what were your feelings towards her?'

Brady piped in at the 'deceiving'. No good. Overruled. Shut the fuck up, Brady. You're holding up the proceedings here.

'She seemed very nice. I wanted to get to know her better.'

'You did not blame her for having placed you in the *care* of Sister Dominic?'

Oh, I meant to say, when Corn sent his collection to art galleries, they printed them in their catalogues

– notoriety gets the punters in I suppose – and Tom Fred had copies. He held up a few.

'These portraits, Picasso's subject matter: nuns in Christian Brother cassocks, replete with belts and crucifixes, portraying androgynously – yet predominantly through the female sex – the evil of which both sexes are capable, is said – as we have heard from an eminent criminal psychologist – to illustrate the background of the artist, his experiences as a child. In particular this one – the Medusa painting. It depicts a nun with two faces, one beautiful, the other – on the back of her head reflected in a mirror – of Medusa. A small boy cowers for protection behind a statue of Christ, which the Medusa face has turned to stone. If such a boy, having suffered maltreatment to the point of insanity, grew to express these experiences by preying *on* the female sex, does it not follow that others who had undergone such maltreatment *might* also be capable of such depraved acts?'

Nah, you're way off the mark there, Tom Fred. I know stacks of people who turned out all right – look at me.

'Did you ever cower behind a statue of Christ, Lucille?'

'Oh, sweet Jesus, please help me. Jesus, please, please help me.' That was Lucille.

'Later to prey on your great-aunts, mother and grandfather to obtain his estate: the idyll denied to you as a baby?'

'No.'

'You have told the court that the most ruthless killer this country has ever known, having held you in a cell, having subjected you to the horrors of almost being eaten alive, then mysteriously – perhaps out of the goodness of his heart – allowed you to go free. How many of Picasso's victims have enjoyed such a reprieve?'

'None.'

Corn's not into reprieves.

'Then why you?'

'I have no explanation.'

'You took lessons at the Donavan riding stables?'

'Yes.'

'Where follicle-inducing stimulants were in the tack room?'

'Yes.'

'Which were used to bring a mare into labour?'

'Yes.'

'To which you had access? Since you took riding lessons there?' A lot of objections and gavel banging going on.

'Which also applied to the ingredients used to make the formalin gas which killed Conor Donavan?'

'Yes.'

'You also told the court that your fingerprints and yours alone were found on the laptop computer used to blackmail Picasso?'

'Yes.'

'That, with the beneficiaries dead, only you, as your mother's and grandfather's closest living relative, stood to benefit?'

231

'Yes.'

And on and on and on. And on. And on.

One reporter wrote that she 'looked pitiful, as if she was in another dimension, an observer in a dream in which others argued over a future she had no say in'. I was hoping he'd write that with Tom Fred on a roll against her, and what with the temperature hitting the eighties, that – for once – she'd taken off those long sleeves she was always wearing and Chill'd copped that birthmark on her arm and realised who she was. I'd've laughed my bollocks off. Still, there are other ways to laugh your bollocks off – not at the verdict: that was always a foregone – four lives each to run concurrently.

'Wanna know what it's like to be up for murders you never committed and sit listening to testimony that proves you did it when all along you know you didn't and you feel like some fucker's tied you to a chair in a target range with a bullseye round your neck and invited anyone with evidence to fire it at you? Yeah? Then you'll have some idea of how your daughter felt? That was her up on the stand, ya daft bastard. Bye, Chill.'

That's how I'd like to have told him. Didn't matter – he'd find out anyway. After I'd been to see my solicitor my name'd be out in the open and Chilly'd be getting a call that'd take his mind back to the day his baby was taken.

'Mr Winters, Conor Donavan's solicitor here. You asked me months ago to notify you if anyone came forward to claim Conor's estate.' Standard cop stuff. 'Well, someone has. And he can prove it.'

232

'Who is he?'

'A Mr Robert Dock.'

'Robert Dock?'

'Yes.'

'*Red* Dock?'

'His solicitor did refer to him as Red, yes.'

'Fuck!'

'Mr Winters are you—'

Down would go the phone.

Up until now, with my name out of the equation, Lucille was seen as just another sorry case who'd bumped off her family to get their money. With my name *in* the equation, all that'd change.

'And all very conveniently after Lucille's been put away for it, who should step forward but Red Dock' would ping away in that brain of his until 'Forget that there's no evidence against him, Red Dock has motive and he's well capable of framing people' told him that Lucille had been a pawn, used, manipulated, all that.

By the time he got round to 'But why frame Lucille? Why *her*? And to frame her, Dock'd have to have known she was a Donavan. How? Even she didn't know till her birth certificate turned up. It was that cert that led her out to Clonkeelin, and within weeks the Donavans were dead. But how reliable is that cert? If Dock's behind this, its authenticity has to be questionable. Is it hers? If not, she's not a Donavan. Then who is she?' The answer'd be on his desk. Thought I'd send him a couple of snapshots – one front-pager showing Lucille fainting when the verdict was read out, another taken by me when she was a baby on the steps of that orphanage I'd taken her to – and a silver St Christopher she'd been wearing round her neck, which I'd kept 'specially for the occasion.

Fuck him. What could he do?

Ask his boss for a retrial?

'No problem, Chill. Let's go see the chimp.'

'Yeah, well, y'see, Your Honour, I've been having a bit of a think.'

'Oh yeah?'

'Lucille's my daughter.'

'You screwed Anne Donavan?'

'No, no, I didn't screw Anne Donavan.'

'Does Lucille know?'

'No.'

'You gonna tell her? Look how she treated her other relatives. Ask Tom Fred.'

'They're not her relatives.'

'But she *thought* they were. The evidence says so.'

'That's because Red Dock set her up.'

'You can prove that?'

'Well, no, I ...'

'Why would he set her up?'

'He hates me.'

'Why?'

'I'm a cop.'

'So's the supe. Dock didn't kidnap *his* daughter.'

'He hasn't got a daughter.'

'You ain't got a daughter?'

'Ah, no, my wife and I couldn't have a ...'

'I didn't know that. Get him t'fuck outta here.'

Again, what could he do? Go and tell Lucille the good news?

'Excellent. Can I go home now?'

'Ah, well, no, not exactly, Lucille. Knowing and proving are two different things.'

'But ...'

'Sorry, I tried to get that fucking judge to listen to reason but he reckons I'm full of bullshit.'

He'd never be able to jigsaw all the pieces into place, but the name Red Dock would tell him he never would. And the best part'd be that he'd have to live with the fact that he'd put his daughter away and could do sweet fuck all about it.

He'd just have to go around like a lunatic until he could figure out some way to invite me in to play with his tape recorder. That's the only way he'd get her freed. And the only person who could help him to invite me was Corn. And whether or not Winters knew it, Corn had shown him exactly how to do it.

You must have noticed it. Tom Fred stuck it in your face, for fuck's sake. The Medusa painting. The boy in it. Who do you think that boy is? Corn painted himself.

Once Winters twigs to that he'll trace the orphanage inspectors who went round those industrial schools, the brothers and sisters who ran them ... He might even go see the bishop. 'Have a look at this painting, Bish. I need to find the setting. Which industrial school was that statue in?'

Somebody's bound to recognise it as the one me and Corn were in.

At one point the majority of prostitutes and prisoners here were ex-industrial school. Tens of thousands of kids went through those places. All he needed was one to put a name to the face in the painting.

Then there were those punters of Gemma's. Corn'd hit on them. And knowing him, he'd go back for a second helping. He might even try for a third. He thought that plan of his was foolproof. But a blackmailing scam only works once. Keep milking it and the guys you're hitting on start to think up get-outs. Successful businessmen aren't successful because they're stupid.

Even if they didn't pay someone to lay in wait for him, his ruse worked only if they didn't go to the law. Because he was playing them two at a time, if one went to the law, the other would be seen as the blackmailer and vice versa. But if *both* went, the law would see through it. They'd tell the pair of them to go to the waste bin as instructed then leave. Corn would think it safe to collect and they'd grab him. Lucille would ID him as Picasso – and, as I say, he'd take me down with him.

Or would he? If I got caught I'd go down for the rest of my natural whether I squealed on Corn or not. Same goes for him.

Here'd be Winters. 'Tell us about Dock's part in this, Corn.'

'In return for?'

'Well, we can ask the judge to drop the charges for those twenty-odd women you scalpeled, but, ah … he's a bit of a funny cunt that judge.'

Corn hates the law and the system as much as I do. We're too much alike. All Winters's likely to get out of him about me is an 'Apropos?'

There was one other threat to me of course, but you already know about it. No point going over it again.

Fuck it. Time to do what I'd spent my life planning since the age of nine.

My brief had arranged for a funeral company to have Sean reburied and I had to show the undertaker to Sean's grave.

After he'd gone, I stayed a while. Nothing worth describing. Just a dump of a cemetery in the grounds of a burnt-down industrial school. St Pat's they called it. Sean's was a well-tended grave. I always visited him regularly and kept it tidy. Five names were on the headstone. A small stone with no space to carve anything but names and dates of death.

A couple of hours and he'd have a nice new casket with brass handles and be laid to rest on the brow of a hill overlooking the cottage we should have been brought up in. Proper headstone with his name, date of birth, date of death, and 'Loving Brother of Robert' carved on it. Just the way he'd like it.

Winters came over. No doubt Conor's solicitor had told him this'd be taking place. I'd caught a glimpse of him inside the chapel ruins, looking up at an old beaded arch. The same one above the statue in Corn's painting. He'd found the setting. Or I'd led him to it. What was left of it anyway. For all the good it'd do him. .

'I've told Lucille who she really is. It's only a matter

237

of time before you and that animal Picasso are taking her place.'

Yeah, well, a matter of time might be a long time getting here, Chill. We all might be in the ground by then.

'Know what gets me, Dock? The methods you used. I always knew you were twisted but getting an animal to kick someone to death, using a slurry pit, poisonous gas ...'

'Know what gets me, Winters? I always knew you were twisted, but getting an animal to kick someone to death, using a slurry pit, poisonous gas... Don't tell me you don't recognise your own part in this. It was you who set the whole thing in motion. Now fuck off out of my way – I've got my brother's funeral to attend to.'

LUCILLE

When Sean Dock was reburied on the Donavan land, an old man came up to my father and said that he'd heard about the funeral and wanted to speak to Robert Donavan. He was told that he hadn't yet arrived.

As the afternoon drew on, the old man explained that he was a friend of Robert Donavan's mother and had been in the cottage the night the twins were born.

In 1949 Mr Donavan senior and his wife Teresa and their three children – Conor, fourteen, Edna, eleven, and Amy, ten – lived in poverty. When Mr Donavan was killed in a farming accident, the priest arrived and took their children away. With no land of her own and her husband gone it wasn't unusual then for the Church to regard women as unable to care for their children. The police took Conor, Edna and Amy to an industrial school.

Some weeks later, Teresa learned that she was pregnant by her husband. She travelled to England to get a job and make a home for herself and her children and returned after seven months to collect them. But the Church wouldn't let them go. The trauma brought her into labour, a Doctor Skeffington was called and the twins were born. He advised a couple of weeks' rest then left. Afraid that the priest would take them, the reason that she'd kept her pregnancy to herself, she wrapped the twins in shawls and took the bus to Dublin to catch the ferry back to England.

Conor went to England before the old man learned he'd been released. And there he stayed, working and searching for his mother.

He returned years later and built the Donavan farm into what it is today. If he'd found Teresa, he'd have found the twins. The old man said he hadn't the heart to tell him he'd lost two brothers as well as a mother. Time, he thought, would bring them back.

Red Dock was found that night in his car, in a byroad less than a mile from the Donavan farm. He'd died from a bullet wound to the head. A man called Kane had been seen parked near the industrial-school cemetery. My father believes that Charlie Swags had him killed because he'd kept his son on remand while he had the evidence to have the charges against him dropped, though it was never able to be proven.

In an upstairs safe in the Copper Jug an old St Patrick's Industrial School enrolment ledger was found. Names in it were traced and Cornelius Hockler was arrested.

He was tried and sent to an institution for the criminally insane.

My father was troubled by what Red Dock had said to him in connection with how Amy, Edna and

Conor Donovan had died. He spoke to those who had known Sean Dock. They told of child slave labour, of Sean Dock being put to work on the farm and almost dying as a result of falling into a slurry pit. He had also worked in a small medal-casting foundry and was once overcome by poisonous fumes. And he was kicked to death by a Christian Brother.

The twins' entry in the ledger records the date they were taken there: 18 October 1949 and their mother: Teresa Donavan, Clonkeelin, Kildare. The first two letters of her surname, 'DO', the 'C' for Clonkeelin and the 'K' for Kildare were underlined in ink. Twins Robert and Sean Donavan: Robert and Sean Dock.

In 1949, when my father was a young constable, he was called to the city hospital. A woman, clutching two babies to her breast, had collapsed on the gangplank of the Liverpool ferry. She was taken to hospital and pronounced dead on arrival. He was handed the few personal belongings she had (they'd been wrapped in brown paper and it was not his place to read them) and told to take her twin sons to the care of an industrial school.

He remembers the conditions with disgust. But, again, it wasn't his place to act.

I asked him whose it was. He didn't answer.

My own belief is this: Red Dock put me in the care of the Church because my father put him and Sean in the care of the Church.

Below the twins' entry was written: 'Brought in by Garda Winters'.

ACKNOWLEDGEMENTS

Huge thanks to my agent Svetlana Pironko. Without S, you wouldn't be reading this.

Big thank you too to Chris Kydd, Laura Nicol, Thomas Ross, Laura Kincaid, big boss Campbell Brown, and all the gang at Black & White Publishing for working their magic.